The Ray Williams Chronicles: High Moon

S.W. McCall

Copyright © 2021 S.W. McCall.

All rights reserved. No part of this publication may be reproduced, distributed, or transmitted in any form or by any means, including photocopying, recording, or other electronic or mechanical methods, without the prior written permission of the publisher, except in the case of brief quotations embodied in critical reviews and certain other noncommercial uses permitted by copyright law. For permission requests, write to the publisher, addressed "Attention: Permissions Coordinator," at the address below.

ISBN: 979-8-78580044-1 (Paperback)
Library of Congress Control Number: 2021925332

Any references to historical events, real people, or real places are used fictitiously. Names, characters, and places are products of the author's imagination.

Front cover image by S.W. McCall.
Book design by S.W. McCall.

First printing edition 2021.

Table of Contents

Chapter 1 Crises in Maple..5
Chapter 2 Red Rock Canyon Memories......................................13
Chapter 3 Shootouts, Mineshafts, and Misfortune.......................20
Chapter 4 Return to Maple...31
Chapter 5 The Fowler Horse Ranch..38
Chapter 6 Tombstone Cemetery..47
Chapter 7 Home Planning, Home Sick, Homefield Advantage......................56
Chapter 8 Old and New Friends..62
Chapter 9 Not Out of the Woods Just Yet....................................73
Chapter 10 Welcome to Saint Edgerton..88
Chapter 11 Hammers, Nails, and Voodoo..................................107
Chapter 12 Escaping the House of Dread..................................133
Chapter 13 Witch Hunt..153
Chapter 14 Ghouls and Nightmares...197
Chapter 15 Ghost Town Showdown...216
Epilogue...250

This book is dedicated to my loving wife Christina, my daughter Ember Rae, and my son Caspian Peter, who continuously encourages me to improve every day. There is nothing you three cannot do if you put your mind to it. This book is also dedicated to my friends Tom H., Jon O., and Connor Q., as you three have consistently encouraged me through the thick and the thin. The three of you keep me on top of my game so that I am always the best me that I can be. Thank you.

This book is in loving memory of my grandmother Orellia "Ricky" McCall, My uncle Dennis Wayne Forrester, and my mother-in-law Deborah Olson. All three of you have left us far too soon, and I miss you three dearly.

Chapter 1 Crisis in Maple

It was high noon on July 2nd of 1889. It seemed just like every other day, but it was more than that. This day would change Ray William's life for the worst. Ray was a bounty hunter and a good one at that. With that being said, sometimes it doesn't matter how good one is at what they do. Sometimes, the odds are just stacked against them.

The day started pretty standard with Ray riding into Maple on Smokey. Smokey was a quarter horse that had grey hair covering its body. His mane was black as coal and flowed majestically in the wind when he ran as quickly as possible. Ray was quite fond of Smokey, as he was a gentle horse and a reliable one. He had never really scared easily in all of the time he had him.

The town of Maple was a pretty unique-looking area. The founders constructed the buildings of brown wooden planks right upon the sand; this acted as their foundation. Sitting in the middle of the right side of town was a massive saloon. This place was always ready for any folks that needed to wet their whistle. The general shop was across the dirt road from all the folks who needed anything else, which is where Ray's family would go to pick up anything they needed when he was young.

    As Ray made it through the town, he ended up following the dirt road directly to the sheriff's office. He found the sturdiest post outside the office, and he hitched Smokey to it. With his horse secured, Ray started making his way up the three-step staircase into the only form of shade that he had all morning. The sheriff's office wasn't much more than a little shack. It shared a lot of similarities to the other buildings in the town as it was almost entirely composed of light brown wooden planks. When Ray walked into the building, it took a moment for his eyes to adjust, as it was bright outside, and the only light that filled the room was a little lantern that sat on the right side of the sheriff's desk. The one window was designed only to allow little light to shine through it. It was almost as if it was built this way to taunt the inmates with a small beacon of freedom that they would never be able to reach. The sheriff's desk sat in the left-back corner of the room was made of the same wood that the office was.

    Directly to the right of the desk was a tiny cell; two walls of it were made of iron bars while the other two walls shared the offices. The cell itself wasn't that big. It could hold one, maybe two people max. At the time, the cell was devoid of all life. The only things were a bench held up with two rusty chains and an old toilet. Cleanliness wasn't a huge focus as the toilet was so stained one could have sworn that it was composed of porcelain mixed with brown obsidian.

Ray walked through the swinging doors into the dimly lit room, seeing two familiar figures having a heated conversation. The shorter man was Sheriff Johnson, an older gentleman, probably in his late fifties. Sheriff Johnson had a kind and seasoned face with wrinkles well earned from his years of wisdom. He wore an old brown cowboy hat with a bullet hole from a recent firefight earlier that year. Ray saw this and thought to himself, "thankfully, that's all the old coot got." Sheriff Johnson also wore a brown vest with a shiny badge attached to the front right part of his uniform. This man was covered from head to toe in dirt, but the thing that Ray always found amusing was that no one would ever see even a speck of dust on his badge.

The other man matched Sheriff Johnson in age and familiarity. His name was Michael O'Brian, and he was the owner of the local general goods store. Michael was a very well-groomed individual with his grey hair greased down and combed neatly to the side. He had a much thinner mustache than the sheriff's; however, based on how neat and symmetrical it was, Ray always assumed he groomed it to look like that. O'Brian's choice of apparel was a long white apron stained with dark brown marks from where Mike would consistently wipe his dirty hands. Under it, he wore a nice white button-up shirt complemented by a black-tie that hung loosely from his neck. It was similar to a lightly tied noose that had been shot down from the middle of the rope. O'Brian's pants were black as coal and seemed to be in pristine condition, and his black shoes shined almost as if trying to steal the spotlight from the sheriff's badge.

"Don't tell me to calm down!" O'Brian's voice shot out as he pointed his thumb into his chest, consistently glaring at the sheriff. "All I'm trying to tell you is that I am on the job, and I ain't going to rest until I find her. Now, I understand that you're worried. Hell, anyone would be, but losing your cool ain't going to help anyone." O'Brian became quiet for a moment, turning away from the sheriff. "I…..I know; it's just she's my baby, my little girl." A single tear dripped from his eye, like the last drop of water trying to sneak its way out of a spigot. Ray intervened with the hopes of being able to assist. "What the hell is going on?" he asked. The sheriff answered while making his way over to O'Brian, placing his hand on his shoulder to console him. "Unfortunately, Mr. O'Brian's daughter, Sarah, was taken by a band of outlaws."

The sheriff paused for a moment, then turned his head away while looking around the room. Most likely due to a combination of discomfort and trying to find the right words to say. "We don't have their names; we don't have any strong eyewitnesses, shit if Mr. O'Brian didn't wake up to the sounds of Sarah screaming, we wouldn't have anything to go off of." Sheriff Johnson let out a tired sigh. "Anyway, this ain't your problem, so what brought you by anyhow, Mr. Williams?" Sheriff Johnson questioned, trying to ensure all was well. Ray responded with his typical response, "Oh, you know, was just looking to see if y'all have any honest work." Sheriff Johnson laughed. "Boy, you are just a glutton for punishment, ain't you?" The reason behind Sheriff Johnson's statement was that Ray had been working side by side with him as a bounty hunter for at least ten years now. Some of the bounties he had brought in wouldn't be considered easy.

Sheriff Johnson paused for a moment, running his left hand over his chin while thinking. "Well, we have a few people you could bring in; however, if you wouldn't mind assisting me with this pressing matter and helping Mr. O'Brian's daughter, I'm sure we could make it worth your while." Mr. O'Brian fell to his knees harder than a sack of grain hitting the ground. His hands clenched together so hard that his knuckles became paler than a ghost, and more tears streamed down his face. "Please, sir, I will personally make it worth your while. Just bring my baby girl home." Mr. O'Brian's eyes were wide as cantaloupes while he stared intently at Ray, waiting for his decision. Ray sort of glared at the sheriff, feeling that he was now in a position where he couldn't help but oblige the offer. "Not a problem Mr. O'Brian." he said, walking to the side of his and placing his hand on his shoulder. "If I am going to find her, I need you to tell me everything that you know."

O'Brian started to recall what little he remembered. "All I remember is saying goodnight to Sarah, then falling asleep." Mike paused for a moment, looking as if he were starting to choke on the words he was trying to say. After a few deep breaths, he was able to continue. "Quicker than thunder filling the sky after a lightning strike, a blood-curdling scream drowned out the silence. I then stumbled down the stairs and outside into the night. With my bare feet becoming submerged into the then muddy sand, I heard a faint daddy help that drowned out the sound of the rain." O'Brian Paused for a moment. His face was grim, "Based on the direction, my daughter's voice was coming from the front door of the shop. Her captors had to have ridden this direction." O'Brian paused for a few seconds, exhaling a sigh, showing his discouragement. Looking him straight in the eye, Ray said, "Don't worry, I'll locate your daughter and have her home by nightfall." O'Brian's eyes became wide, and he rushed over to Ray, grabbing his hand. His grip was tighter than a python constricting prey, yet shakier than a leaf in mid-fall.

    Once Ray's hand was freed, he tilted his hat toward Mr. O'Brian and headed to where Smokey was hitched. Sheriff Johnson told Mr. O'Brian, "Give me a moment. I'm going to walk Ray out, and I will be right back." O'Brian just nodded and looked down while Sheriff Johnson walked out the doors, down the stairs to where Ray was working on unhitching his horse. Making it to talking distance, Sheriff Johnson explained that based on what Mr. O'Brian told him, it sounded like the outlaws responsible for abducting Sarah were headed toward Red Rock Canyon; if it were up to him, he would start there. Ray slid his right boot into one of Smokey's stirrups; this allowed him to bring his other leg up over to the horse. He then utilized the reins to steady himself on him. Once he was confident he wasn't going to fall, he thanked Sheriff Johnson for his information, guided Smokey down the road toward the canyon, and let out a resounding "Hiyah!" as a trail of dust followed them like their shadows.

Chapter 2 Red Rock Canyon Memories

It had to have been about two hours later when Ray finally reached the Red Rock Canyon. The canyon's name described it well, as the walls were made of a pale red combination of iron oxidized boulders and clay. The walls were so high that any manufactured tower would have been put to shame by its might. The canyon's ground looked similar to the dirt trail Ray had ridden in on but with a slightly deeper red tint, likely due to the dust of the wall mixing into it due to natural erosion. As Ray followed the trail into the canyon, the walls ascended around him. He heard only Smokey's hooves hitting the dirt as they consistently echoed through the walls. The only thing he could think about was his love, Elaine Emmerson, and what led him up to this point.

Elaine was young and a lady in every sense of the word. Her hair was such a bright blond that when the sun hit it just right, one could not help but mistake it for gold. Elaine's eyes were a light baby-blue color, which put the ocean to shame in comparison. Her smile had a way of entrancing any man lucky enough to get a glimpse. She was a gentle soul who always would try to go out of her way to better her fellow man. When she was eighteen, she decided to pursue higher education in Fine Arts, thus relocating to a college for women. Four years later, Elaine finished her degree. It was then that she decided to relocate back to Maple, where Ray met her.

The day started similar to any other, with Ray finishing up some chores. He was in town shopping for supplies at O'Brian's shop that day. Shortly after grabbing everything needed, Ray took it out to Smokey and secured it to the back of his trusty steed. With it tied, he tugged on it a few times to ensure that it wouldn't budge and then started unhitching him. With Smokey loose, Ray pulled himself onto his back and rode off, leaving a trail of dust in his tracks. Thankfully, Ray lived in the outskirts of town on the same side as the general goods store, past the old train tracks. This was incredibly convenient when he had to stop in and pick things up as he didn't have to ride to the other side of town.

As he was heading home, he made it only a few feet from the train tracks before coming to a sharp halt. A young woman was pacing back and forth in the train station with a look of severe distress across her face. She was wearing a baby-blue dress with little strips of white at the bottom, sleeves, and around the neck. She also wore a baby-blue bonnet to match a white flower entangled in part of the thread. Being the kind of guy always to try to help when he could, Ray rode Smokey over to the edge of the wooden floor of the train station, relatively close to where Elaine was waiting. "Howdy, ma'am," Ray said with a slightly forced deep voice. Elaine's eyes met his, causing his heart to race and him to feel like his body temperature was hotter than an Arizona summer. A slight smile came across her lips as Ray continued, "I ain't trying to be a Nosy Parker, but I could see that something looked wrong." Elaine responded with a high pitch southern accent, "No, you're fine, sir. I am a little flustered; you see, one of my family's servants was supposed to pick me up around an hour ago, but there is still no sign of them. Oh, what am I to do?" The troubled look reemerged. "No worries, ma'am." he responded, his voice as deep as before. "I'll take you home."

    Ray reached his hand down in front of Elaine. After a brief moment of hesitation, she placed her hand upon his, hoisting herself upon Smokey's saddle. Settling onto the saddle, Elaine sarcastically teased Ray with a slight grin on her face. "So what name can a damsel call her hero?" Ray pulled his hat down over his eyes to block the sun a little bit better, "You can call me Ray, Ray Williams. And what do you do, ma'am?" She responded, "Elaine, Elaine Emmerson." What was a day's ride felt like minutes. Every second that passed, they learned more about each other and slowly became more attracted.

Then the moment came when they finally reached her home. The house was a massive Victorian-style mansion that looked as if constructed entirely from bricks. The exception to this was the window shutters and the porch, which looked as if they were made of some maroon-colored wood. The mansion sat on many acres of land, which contained stables, animals, and even two barns. Once Smokey finally made it next to the porch, Ray jumped down from his steed and hitched him to a railing along the front of it. He then placed a hand out for Elaine to assist her down. She put her left hand in his while Ray gently lifted her down. He then walked alongside her to her door. Ray softly stated that it was a pleasure and thanked her for her company, to which she replied, "No need to thank me, thank you for being a gentleman." At that moment, Ray started back toward his horse only to have Elaine's soft hands snatch his rough ones up, leading him inside and up into her sleeping quarters.

 Ray spotted something odd after riding around for hours, which quickly brought him out of his thoughts. Deep within the canyon, an old mine shaft had approximately nine or ten black stallions hitched outside it. Along with them sat an old Conestoga wagon that had about a dozen bullet holes along the side of the cover. Ray wondered how they could get the wagon here or how long it had been sitting there as the front wheel seemed busted and missing around three to four of the wooden planks that were the foundation.

 Ray rode to the wagon's side that faced away from the mine shaft opening. A small, crooked Fremont cottonwood tree caught his eye in this area. Ray then slid off his horse, grabbed the reins, and led him to the tree, hitching him. After giving the rope an extra tug to ensure that Smokey was securely fastened, Ray ran his hand along the side of the saddle and pulled his shotgun out of its dark leather scabbard, hanging it with its strap around his shoulder.

 The shotgun was a Remington 1889 model that Ray picked up from an outlaw that attacked him during his last bounty hunt. The gun was a double-barrel made with Damascus Steel, while wood from a walnut tree was used to compose the weapon's stock and other accenting parts. The one thing that stood out about this gun was a poorly carved outline of a wolf's head along with a couple of knicks where Ray missed when cutting into it with his knife, located on the middle of the right side of the gun's stock. Ray always likes to personalize his firearms, and this shotgun was no exception. The final touch to his personalization was always naming it. For this gun, Ray chose to call it the Silver Wolf, as the steel looked like silver, and the shot from it would surround any prey in front of it, much like a pack of wolves.

    The following weapons that Ray retrieved were his two revolvers. With both in hand, he slid one into a holster on his left side and one into a holster on his right. Each handgun was a Colt Peacemaker composed of coal-black metal from the barrel to the hammer. On the other hand, the grip was made of a pale, smoothed-out wood that matched the color of a Yellowwood tree. Each revolver had an engraving of an eagle swooping down toward the barrel. These were found on opposite sides of the grips, making them the perfect pair. The two Peacemakers were Ray's most prized guns, as they have been incredibly reliable in bad situations and due to their style. Ray ended up naming them "The Birds of Prey." Double-checking to make sure he wasn't leaving anything of importance behind, Ray loaded up and took a few deep breaths as he snuck his way around the wagon and secured his back right along the mineshaft entrance. Ray pulled out his Birds of Prey, placing them on his chest and one more big deep breath. Once ready, Ray yelled into the mineshaft, "Where is she, you sons of bitches?"

Chapter 3 Shootouts, Mineshafts, and Misfortune

Ray's only response to his inquiry was an echo that started to fade out. Ray leaned in, yelling one more time. "I ain't asking again!" He met with multiple bullets flying through the air this time, just barely missing his head. The gunfire caused Ray to press his body against the wall, utilizing it as cover. His heart was beating so hard; it felt like it was going to pop out of his chest. A deep, faint voice could be heard laughing from within the shaft, "If you want her, then come get her." Ray peeked around the corner seeing two guys. One was closer, leaning along the edge of the stone wall, while the other one was crouched back behind what seemed to be a giant crate.

Ray took a deep breath in an attempt to keep calm. Once he completely exhaled, Ray shot each Bird of Prey revolver three times. The gun in his left hand filled the wooden box with holes, while the one in the right hand hit the stone wall with the first two shots. The third shot from the right revolver pierced the closer guy's skull. His lifeless body fell to the floor while the guy behind the crate proceeded to fire two more shots toward Ray. The first one chipped a piece of wood off the foundation, which was in place to secure the opening of the mineshaft, while the other one whizzed past Ray's ear. Ray peaked his gun around the corner and took another shot; this time, the guy behind the crate was peeking over it. The bullet that Ray shot ended up digging into the outlaw's skull, scoring him another headshot. Ray slowly descended into the mineshaft, staying alert for anyone who may rush out of the cave in response to the gunfire. Making his way to where the bodies lay, he proceeded to pat down both of the corpses for any loot that he could find. The entire time he was doing this, he kept his eyes locked onto the dark path in front of him.

    Ray continued down the path; each step became more consumed by darkness. The cause of this seemed to be due to the lanterns and torches getting spread farther and farther apart the further he descended. What felt like thirty minutes to an hour later, Ray came across an opening on the side of the tunnel, which revealed a massive room that the miners had gutted out. From Ray's position, he could see two tunnels. One ran from the left side of the room, and the other ran to the back right corner. Both tunnels seemed to be connected with minecart tracks, which ran through the middle of the massive room. Looking down, Ray noticed that there were minecart tracks on the ground that led down the tunnel. Seeing this, Ray realized that the route he was descending led into the massive room, and they had to be connected.

Ray crouched down and quickly attempted to run to the other side of the big opening. Before he made it over, his hat flew off, and a loud clinging sound could be heard hitting the wall. Ray jumped back to the side where he was previously standing, only to have a barrage of bullets hitting where he once was crouched. Quickly, he pulled out the Birds of Prey revolvers, opened up the chambers, reloaded each gun, and jumped out to the opening. He then fired six shots through the air; only two of them made contact with the outlaws, piercing each of them through their skulls. The wounds caused both outlaws to drop like rocks in a lake. The sound of gunfire thundered through the cavern as the remainder of the bullets ended up making contact with the wall. Some of the outlaws started firing back, which in turn caused Ray to jump back to the side that he was previously hiding behind.

With his back pressed against the cold wall, intense pain shot through the side of his left knee. Sliding down till he was sitting on the floor, he slipped his revolver that was in his left hand back into its holster. With his hand now empty, he quickly placed it over the stinging sensation. The pain from his touch caused it to sharpen, so naturally, Ray instinctively jerked his hand back. Looking over it, he noticed that his hand was covered in blood. A look of irritation consumed his face as he muttered to himself, "Son of bitch." Down the tunnel to his left, the sound of a gun cocking could be heard echoing off of walls. Within seconds, Ray slid his other revolver into its holster and brought his Silver Wolf shotgun to the ready in a fluid motion. Preparing himself for anyone who thought he was easy prey.

    Two men ascended from the tunnel, running toward him. One was holding an old repeater. It looked as if it had been poorly maintained. It also looked like it had been kept out in the rain, as it was rusted all to hell. The other man was holding a double-barrel shotgun which seemed to be in a similar condition. Ray aimed his gun between the two men and pulled the trigger. The bullets surrounded them with a loud bang like a swarm of pissed-off bees. This caused each of them to scream as they flew backward, ending their lives swiftly.

Ray placed the shotgun along the wall for a moment and unsheathed his knife. He pulled his sleeve back and used the knife to cut off a good portion of it. Once wholly separated from the rest of his shirt, he tied it tight around his leg wound to assist with slowing down on the bleeding. Ray then slid his knife back in its sheave, placed the shotgun back in its holster, and recalled the Birds of Prey revolvers. Before having a chance to move further down the tunnel, another two outlaws headed toward Ray, firing a barrage of bullets toward him. Once both men cease-fired to reload, Ray peeked around the corner and took a couple of shots at them with his revolvers. The two outlaws ended up running behind a large wooden crate for cover and immediately began open firing in Ray's direction. Ray yelled out, taunting them, "Your shooting makes y'all seem like you couldn't tell skunks from house cats!"

The men stopped firing again to reload, and Ray noticed that one of the few lanterns that lit the tunnels hung directly above the crate they were hiding behind. Closing one eye, he raised his left revolver's barrel toward the light and pulled the trigger. The bullet zipped through the air, nicking the lantern's handle. This caused the lantern to fall directly onto the edge of the wooden crate, shattering as the glass made contact with the wood. As the lantern exploded, fire rained upon both outlaws, and they could be heard shrieking in immense pain for a few seconds. The sounds subsided quickly and were replaced instead by dead silence.

Clearing the small tunnel, Ray pulled himself up and limped through the dim tunnel. Quickly, he made his way over to the two charred bodies of the fools that tried to kill him. When Ray looted them for whatever was salvageable, he couldn't help but cringe as his nostrils became filled with a scent that smelled similar to pork cooking in an iron skillet, seasoned with charcoal and sulfur. Ray's search was in vain because the fire damaged any item he did find. Ray continued stumbling along the mine cart tracks until he found himself in another dimly lit tunnel. With his revolvers at the ready, he continued carefully down the decently long tunnel. At the end, it took a sharp turn to the right. Eventually, this led him into the big, open area that he saw earlier in the tunnel.

The massive room was surprisingly quiet. Ray assumed it was due to most of the men that filled it attempting to rush him in the tunnel. Constantly looking around to ensure he was ready for an ambush, he continued to follow the minecart tracks into the other tunnel that merged into the massive room. Unlike the previous one, this tunnel was significantly shorter. Ray thought it weird that there was a poorly built door made of wooden planks at the end of it. This door had a few massive gaps in it that the dim light from the other side couldn't help but shine through.

    Ray made his way to the door, pressing his body against the ruff wooden panels, and then started to push it slowly. This pressure caused the door to release a loud creaking sound gradually. With the door opening, Ray could peek inside the small room. One of the things that seemed weird was that the minecart tracks ended right where the room's door meant the tunnel. Once the door was completely open, Ray could see the shopkeeper's daughter. She was a young girl, mid-twenties, with blonde hair. The girl's clothing was dirty and tattered but not destroyed. The shopkeeper's daughter's hands were bound with rope as she was unconsciously hanging from them off one of the lantern hooks.

    Ray stumbled his way across the floor over to the girl. This was when he placed two fingers on her carotid artery to see if he could catch a pulse. After a few seconds, he let out a sigh of relief upon uncovering it. Both of the Birds of Prey slipped into their proper holsters as Ray unsheathed his old rusty hunting knife. He then started to run the blade across the rope with his right hand while he utilized his left arm to hold up the shopkeeper's daughter in hopes of preventing her from falling when he finished cutting. What must have been seconds felt like an hour as Ray's blade finally made its way through most of the rope. He decided to re-position himself in fear of not having a good enough grip on her, for when she fell. As Ray moved his injured leg back, he crouched down a little bit on his good leg in preparation for whatever direction she fell. He did this in hopes of giving him a higher point of leverage, but before he could follow through, something heavy jumped on Ray's back. Pain from the bullet wound shot through Ray's leg, causing him to collapse to one knee and let out an agonizing scream. His wail of pain was cut short as two sharp fangs entered his neck. Ray attempted to swing back with his knife, but whatever this thing was, it grabbed his wrist. Ray felt himself getting weaker by the second. The figure's grip was tighter than a python's, his hand was tombstone cold, and the bite stung more than a viper's venom.

The being finally released its cold embrace, and Ray collapsed completely to the floor. His knife slid over to the wall. He then utilized all of his might to force himself to roll over weakly. His eyesight was going in and out of focus like he suddenly developed astigmatism. The being was standing directly above him at this point. The only lantern in the room hung behind the figure, making it difficult to see his face. Ray made out the outline of an old cowboy hat, a trench coat, and a dark blood-covered smile painted across his face. "I wouldn't try anything funny." The creature stated in a raspy voice that it sounded similar to a rattle snake's rattle. Ray pulled out his right revolver, aimed it at the beast, and fired off a shot. However, this was to no avail as the creature didn't seem even a little phased by it. The wide grin got wider, "Don't you understand, boy? You can't hurt me." The menacing words seeped out of his mouth. The being slowly made its way to Ray's side and kneeled next to him on one of its knees. It proceeded to grab him by the cheeks, forcing open his mouth. Then, the figure swished around something in his mouth and spit it into Ray's. The taste of iron covered his tongue, which after being hit in the mouth a couple of times in the past, Ray quickly figured out that it was blood. This led him to try to spit it out immediately, but, unfortunately, he was unable due to the figure's grip on his cheeks and how weak he was at this point. After a second of struggling, Ray started coughing, which caused him to swallow all of the contaminates that filled his mouth. Suddenly, the world started spinning for Ray, and the figure kept going in and out of focus. Its grin was as wide as it could get. This is when Ray's head fell to the floor from exhaustion, and he lost consciousness.

    To Ray, this loss of consciousness felt like he blinked; however, the girl and the beast were gone when he opened his eyes. Still weakened from the whole endeavor, Ray started rocking his body back and forth to roll over on his stomach, letting out slight grunts of pain with every move. Due to the momentum of the third rock to the right, he finally achieved his goal of reaching his stomach. "Where the hell did that son of a bitch go?" Ray mumbled as he attempted to bring himself to his knees. Due to his lack of energy, Ray just collapsed back onto his stomach, cringing his face in sync with his pain. "Well, it looks like the only way I'm getting out of here is like a damned snake," Ray told himself weakly as he picked up the revolver that lay on the ground next to him, struggling to slip it into his holster. He then started dragging himself slowly toward the entrance.

Halfway up the tunnel, Ray noticed that the light from the lantern was causing a glimmer to shine off of something lying next to the outlaw's corpse that held the rusty shotgun. Ray didn't remember seeing it on his way down into the lower parts of the mine shaft, so he figured it could be a clue, incentivizing him to pick it up on his way out. After crawling a few feet forward, Ray was finally able to pick up the item; it turned out to be a pocket watch. Due to his overwhelming injuries, Ray decided to look at it later. He slid the pocket watch into his leather pouch. Ray then resumed his crawl to the entrance of the mine shaft. Minutes felt like hours as Ray finally reached his destination to see all the horses, including his own, gone. "Shit." Ray thought to himself as the realization that this might be his last bounty crossed his mind. Seconds later, Ray's body collapsed to the ground thanks to exhaustion, and the world went dark.

Chapter 4 Return to Maple

Much like the last time Ray lost consciousness, it felt like mere seconds; however, this wasn't the case. Once his eyes finally opened, he saw a man with a familiar face staring down at him. The man's name was Doc Mathews, and he was Maple's town doctor. Doc was a pretty easy face to remember as he had short, black, thick, wavy hair that swept to the right in conjunction with a Van Dyke mustache style that complimented it. As for Doc's attire, he was always wearing a nice pair of black dress pants, a white dress shirt, and a black tie to accent it. He was a middle-aged man who wore a lot of his experience on his face, and his brown eyes were kind while serious.

"Are you ok?" Doc asked. "I'm fine," Ray stated shortly, letting out a deep breath and slowly sitting himself up. "So, how exactly did I end up here?" Doc sat down in a chair close to where he was standing. "A local trader was on his way into town and saw you unconscious, sprawled out like a snake. And rather than leaving you for the vultures, he loaded you up in his caravan and brought you here." Ray cautiously pulled himself up to his feet. A bolt of pain shot through his left leg, which caused his hands to rush down to the area. When it hit him, he had an actual bandage covering his wound. Doc proceeded to fill Ray in. "I took a look at your leg while you were unconscious, removed the bullet, and bandaged it up for you. Based on the condition, it should be ok. I am, however, concerned with those puncture wounds that are on your neck. What happened?" Ray attempted to cover up his neck with his collar, "I thank you for your help Doc, but I am good now." Doc had a slightly annoyed look due to Ray brushing off his question, "So how much do I owe you?" Doc's eyes looked to his upper right as if reaching to the back of his mind to search for the answer. "Due to the ointment to fight infection, supplies, and removal of the bullets, I would say fifteen dollars. However, I would suggest waiting around for a little bit so I can make sure you're good. You seem a little pale." Ray scoffed at him. "Yeah, and give you more of the money I don't have?" Ray opened up his tote and rummaged around in it for a moment, took out fifteen dollars, and handed it to Doc. "Listen Doc, I ain't trying to be rude, I do appreciate the concern, but I'm fine." He then reached his hand out toward Doc to shake it, and Doc slowly obliged. "Ray, I understand your hesitation, but just know I am trying to help you." Ray laughed as he started limping toward the exit. "If you want to help, why don't you wet my whistle."

Ray walked outside and decided that a drink would help numb the pain, so he hobbled over to the right, which led to the town's local saloon. The name of the establishment was the Silver Bullet Saloon. The building was laid out in a way that made the front narrow, but with each step further in the establishment, the walls expanded until they made contact with the ends of the bar. The building was built from maple wood like the rest of town, while the bar was Mahogany. Ray made his way through the swinging doors. He noticed a few tables scattered around the floor, each one containing two to three chairs. There were four windows that Ray also saw, two on the right of the swinging doors and two on the left. All four of them had the word "Saloon" plastered across them. On the edge of the window frame to the right sat a grand piano that seemed to be in pristine condition as it had no nicks or scratches, and it looked like the saloon purchased it recently. The wooden swinging doors just added more charm to the establishment, as anytime a person would go through them, the doors would almost flutter like an American Goldfinch would in its attempt to find a mate. The only other patrons were two folks sitting around one of the tables. One of them had a long grey beard and wore a grey cowboy hat with a long grey shirt accented with a set of overalls. The other was a little harder to make out as he had his face buried into his arms.

Ray made his way to the old barkeep, who had a slight smile showing through his chevron-style mustache. The bartender wore a black top hat of similar color to the bow tie, which was tied ever so snug around the neck of the long white dress shirt. "What will it be, sir?" the barkeep asked with a German accent. "I'd like to order whiskey on the rocks, and what do you got for food?" The barkeep rubbed his chin for a second while thinking, "Well, we could make you a burger or something. However, today's complimentary meal is smoked herring and potato chips. Ray stated that he would take it, and the barkeep got to work without any hesitation.

While waiting for his refreshments, Ray pulled the pocket watch out of his pouch. Looking it over, he noticed an engraving on the inside of the lid. The engravement spelled out T.A. Fowler. He started looking around, his mind working "Fowler?" He questioned softly. "Why does that name sound familiar?" The bartender made his way back over to Ray with that cold glass of dark liquor in the right hand and a plate of fish and chips in the other. "Did you say Fowler?" he asked. Ray slowly nodded yes, caught off guard by the observation. The bartender picked up on his hesitation. "I didn't mean to be rude; I just thought that I may be able to help you out, friend. You see, A Fowler is a regular patron here, comes in here consistently." Ray placed the chilled glass against his lips and sipped on the smooth beverage, his eyes not once leaving the bartender. He continued, "If you are looking for a Fowler, I believe one of them owns a ranch between here and that town north of here, Appleton. If nothing else, it would be a good place to start." Ray nodded. "Thank you, friend; I will check it out." The bartender just smiled. "No problem, If you need anything else, just let me know." The barkeep made his way over to the back room, which was concealed visually but had to be close enough to be able to hear the water and clanging of dishes.

Ray's eyes then shifted focus to his food. He tore a piece of the fish off, placing it in his mouth. The flavor was a combination of smoked and salty flavors that competed for dominance but were not too overly aggressive to ruin the taste. Ray took a few bites, and he quickly realized that he wasn't that hungry. It was causing him to become green, causing him to abstain from his meal. Ray placed his hand in his satchel and rummaged around through it, eventually pulling out a few dollar bills and a few coins, putting them next to the mainly unconsumed food. He pulled himself away from the side of the bar and started walking toward the doors.

  Once Ray was outside, he headed to the right toward the train station. Just outside to the train station's left was a stagecoach driver who was for hire. Ray strolled over to him and asked: "How much would be for a ride, friend?" The coach driver smiled and asked how far. "I believe it's about halfway to Appleton." Ray said, his facial expression showing his confidence in his answer. The stagecoach driver stroked his chin for a moment, thinking out loud. "Well, Appleton is around ten miles north of here, so we are talking around five miles." His eyes looked around wildly while calculating the cost in his head. " That's gonna run you sixty cents." Ray accepted the terms, pulled the sixty cents out of his pouch, and hobbled over to the door on the left side of the carriage. He held a small handle attached to its outside and used it to leverage himself up. Ray then used his right hand to open the carriage's door while using the handle previously used for leverage to guide himself into it. Once inside, he sat himself down on one of the two wooden bench seats of the carriage and closed the door. The operator then snapped the reins, and the two chestnut-colored horses headed north.

Chapter 5 The Fowler Horse Ranch

"We are here!" the driver's voice rang through the carriage as it came to a complete stop. Ray looked out the window to see a medium-sized ranch in the distance. "That has to be it," he thought as his eyes squinted, attempting to see it a little better as the heat distortion made it hard to pick up on specific details. Ray pulled himself out of the carriage, thanked the driver again for his assistance, and asked him to meet him back in about an hour or two. "Not a problem." the driver joyfully said as he turned the wagon around and headed back south.

Ray then proceeded to make his way over to the ranch. After about ten minutes, he made it over to the big, light brown, wooden gate that guarded the dirt road which led up to the stables and home. There was a sign that read "Fowler's Ranch," which seemed a little small compared to the remainder of the gate. Connected to the other sides of the gate were light-colored wooden posts that stood from the ground, roughly three feet apart from each other. In-between each one of the posts, three planks of wood were placed horizontally, each with large enough gaps to crawl through if needed but did an excellent job at keeping bigger things, such as caravans or cattle, on the side, they were meant to be. The pattern of these wooden posts could be seen wrapping around the entire ranch as Ray made his way down the dirt road toward the house.

Finally, at the end of the extensive driveway, Ray discovered it evolved into a massive dirt circle. At the edge of it, toward the top left area, sat a single-story log cabin that looked like it was composed of oak wood due to it being a lighter color. The only parts of the home that were not composed of wood were the shingles on the roof, the fireplace that came off of the right side of the cabin, and a little lantern that hung neatly by the door. Ray made his way onto the broad porch and knocked against the door two times. After waiting a few minutes with no response, he started to make his way over to one of the single-hung windows directly to the left of the door. Noticing dust covered it, Ray wiped it off and placed his face against it.

"Hello?" he yelled, flustered by the idea that nobody might be home. Moments later, an older woman burst through the door, wielding a shotgun. "What the hell do you want, Piggy?" Her voice was stern and unweaving. Ray stepped back in confusion and threw his hands in the air, displaying surrender. "Piggy?" he asked. "Who the hell is Piggy?" Without hesitation, she pumped her shotgun. It was an 1889 model just like Ray's but in a different color. "You are! Now tell me what the hell you are doing here, or I am going to turn you to swiss cheese." Their eyes never left each other. "Ma'am, I don't want no trouble," he continued calmly. "I just found this pocket watch, and I was hoping that you could tell me a little bit more about it." Her eyes squinted as if trying harder to analyze Ray for any tricks, "Do you take me for a fool? Why the hell would you come out here to ask an old lady about a pocket watch? And to top that, why the fuck would you think I know anything about pocket watches anyway?"

Ray's hands started to quiver from exhaustion. "Honestly, Ma'am, I didn't expect you to know a ton about pocket watches. However, this one has an engraving on it that spells out T.A. Fowler, and with Fowler being your ranch's name, I figured that this would be a good place to start." Her demeanor shifted. "Oh, I see." She lowered the shotgun barrel and stood by the side of the door, holding it open for Ray. "I'm sorry for the way I acted; things have been crazy lately." She waved her free hand, gesturing to him to come inside. "No shit, lady." Ray thought to himself before he accepted her non-verbal offer. Even with almost being target practice, he still obliged her request and strolled into the home after a moment of slight hesitation.

As he walked past the door, Ray was greeted by two green couches that sat directly across from one another; the only thing separating them was a small coffee table that was wedged in the small gap between them. The walls were the same color and condition as the outside of the cabin. The floor was hardwood which broke off into different hallways. Ray could see the destination of the one that went straight back. It went into the kitchen. The only reason he could tell this was when he looked back there; he could make out the side of the stove. As for the other hallway that went to the left, Ray was unsure of what was on the other end. The lady walked toward the hallway that led to the kitchen, placed the shotgun against the living room wall, and told Ray to have a seat. He obliged and collapsed on the couch facing the hallway that she went into so he could watch the lady the moment she re-emerged from her destination.

The woman carried a black as coal cast iron teapot and two coffee mugs. She placed all the items down on the table in their respective places and asked Ray if he would like some tea, to which he politely declined. "Suit yourself." the lady said, tilting the teapot allowing the hot liquid to pour into her cup. Ray's curiosity and impatience got the better of him. "So ma'am, who exactly is T.A. Fowler?" Without looking up from the tea, she said, "Travis Anthony Fowler is his name, and he was my husband." She placed the cup of tea up to her lips and took a sip. "Was?" Ray asked, "What happened?"

The woman let out a deep breath as she explained. "He rode in from Maple one night, not looking the greatest. I thought he had just painted his tonsils a little too much, but it turned out to be much more. Ray suddenly started having a small coughing fit, catching both of them off guard. "Sorry, ma'am, I wasn't trying to be rude." Ray reassured her as he looked into her eyes. He noticed that the concerned look didn't leave her face. "How long have you had that cough?" she sternly asked. Ray's became even more thrown off by the question. "I haven't had it before; this is my first time." The older lady chimed in again, "Well, you best keep an eye on it, that; this it sounded when my husband Travis first came homesick." she continued, "Anyway, it started with a cough in conjunction with some chest pain. He eventually grew pale, spitting up blood and eventually had to be buried." A consequent grimace came across her face from her past, haunting her.

Mrs. Fowler's eyebrows scrunched up again as something was bothering her. "Come to think of it; he was buried at the Tombstone Cemetery with this watch." She paused for a moment. "How did you get it again?" Ray finally regained his composure from his coughing with the help of a few deep breaths. "Honestly, ma'am, I'm a bounty hunter, and while out on a job, I found the watch on the ground. With that being said, one of the bandits that were there had," Mrs. Fowler interrupted, screaming, "Don't fucking lie to me! You're a damn grave robber, aren't you?!". Ray, completely caught off guard by this, chuckled in disbelief. "No ma'am, I done told you, I ain't a damn grave robber, I'm a bounty hunter." She proceeded to get up, "You're a liar, that's what you are." Ray noticed that she started walking quickly toward the shotgun. In response to this, he swiftly rose himself up and threw himself toward the gun, sliding onto the back of his shoulder as he snatched it up. Ray pointed it at the crazy lady while still lying on his back. Her hands flew up into the air, "You don't have to do this." her nerves presented themselves in a shaky voice. "Dammit, lady, will you fucking listen to me!" Ray started to lose his temper. "I done told you I ain't no fucking grave robber. Now I'm going to go, and I am taking this gun with me. The last thing I need is to be shot in the back by some damn looney woman!" Mrs. Fowler had her hands in the air and was shaking out of angst, tears poured down her cheeks from her eyes. "Please," she begged desperately. With the shotgun in hand, Ray turned around and made his way to the door.

While he was treading forward, he heard the older lady's feet pattering off down the hall in the other direction. Ray made his way through the door and down the porch to the big, dirt driveway. Standing there, he looked down the road to see if the coach driver had made his way back yet. Unfortunately, there was no sight of it. While he was standing there, he thought about just starting to walk back into town, but that would take forever. "Wait a second; this is a horse ranch, ain't it?" Ray thought to himself. Maybe they got a horse I could borrow. Ray started toward the big red barn with white accents that sat directly across the cabin.

"Die, You son of a bitch!" Ray heard as he turned around to see Mrs. Fowler swinging a knife toward him with all of her might. Completely caught off guard, Ray stumbled backward, and after the fourth swing, she threw her body forward to shorten the gap between them. Alas, the lady ended up tripping on her long white nightgown and falling to the dirt. While in mid-fall, her reflexes kicked in, and she threw her hands toward the ground attempting to decrease the impact of her fall. In turn, she failed to release the knife, causing her to impale herself as her body hit the ground. Mrs. Fowler's face let out the expression of pain, and one could tell she tried to scream but only released silence. As seconds passed, a puddle of red seeped from her wound, and her eyes went from frantic to still. Ray then had a chill run up and down his spine as he heard what sounded like whispers coming from where the body lay; however, there was no one there. The whispers were so faint; he could not make out anything that was being said. This eventually caused him to shrug it off, thinking it may just be the wind.

 Ray started making his way back toward the barn, placed his hands against both doors, and pushed them open. Once inside, Ray only found one horse. It was a chestnut-colored Arabian with white accents around the feet and the top of the nose, along with a long beautiful black mane. Ray made his way over to the stable. Hanging off the edge of the top plank of wood, he found a fine leather saddle along with the harness hanging from the saddle's horn. Seizing both, he made his way into the stable while the horse folded his ears back as he backed into the far corner. "Awww, don't you worry, I ain't gonna hurt you." Ray reassured the horse as he started slowly walking toward it. His hands were up in the air, reaching out toward the steed. With every step closer, the horse became more uneasy. This could be seen due to the horse pressing its body closer to the back corner as it stomped its hooves into the dirt rapidly. Ray just continued forward slowly. Cautiously, he slowly made his way over to the horse until it was close enough that he was able to place his hand on his muzzle. Using his right hand, Ray petted him while speaking softly for a few minutes, and it seemed to calm down finally. With the steed soothed, Ray fit the harness on him in conjunction with the saddle. He grabbed the reins and led the horse out of the stable toward the big dirt circle. "I think I will call you Old Red," Ray said as he saddled up. The horse dashed through the gate and headed back toward Maple within seconds.

Chapter 6 Tombstone Cemetery

It was a little after nightfall by the time Ray reached Tombstone Cemetery. The moon was towering over the landscape, causing all graves to cast shadows over the inhabitants' former selves. The cemetery was built upon a lot of land Ray could only get a limited view of due to the surrounding metal Victorian-style fencing keeping him out. With it being on the outskirts of Maple, the cemetery shared the same sand as the town.

Sliding off of Old Red and hitching him to outside the cemetery's fence, Ray pulled the reins to ensure the horse was secured, and he cautiously walked through the cemetery gates. Now Ray was never one who feared the dark or anything along those lines. He was, however, worried that someone would find him and report him as a grave robber. While he and the sheriff have always had a good relationship, he realized that this would be hard to explain if confronted. Each step was guided by a combination of the moon's brightness and the faint outline of the dirt trail. Repurposing the light from the moon also allowed him to read the faint outlines on the graves. Finally, after what seemed like hours, he stumbled across a grave that read

Travis Anthony Fowler 1853 - 1889 beloved husband, son, and brother. The burial site was similar to others surrounding it. The headstone was made of fieldstone, and the opening was filled with rocks and sand. Taking a closer look, Ray noticed that the stones that covered the top of this particular grave seemed to be shuffled around and relatively loose compared to the others.

He wondered for a moment, "What if," as he kneeled to the right of it and started moving the loose stones off of the grave, tossing them to the side. Roughly around fifteen minutes of digging with his hands, he uncovered the top of a wooden coffin. "What the hell am I doing?" Ray paused for a moment, disgusted with the fact that he was defacing a grave. He started to second-guess his decision. "This man is dead. Maybe someone robbed him a long time ago and stole this when he was alive. Or maybe those damn outlaws robbed his grave." Ray paused for a moment and sighed, "On the other hand, I've come this far, all I gotta do is pry open the lid, and I will have a surefire answer." Ray unsheathed his knife and placed it between the lid and the coffin in the crevasse. To his surprise, the top came up without even a little fight, and it was emptier than a killer's heart. Ray stepped back in shock, just trying to make sense of the situation. "How could he have been buried but still be roaming?" he asked himself.

    The wind picked up, causing what few leaves there were to begin rustling. Ray's heart raced, swearing that he heard someone as he threw the lid back onto the coffin and took a step away. "Who's there!?" he yelled as he readied his right revolver, and his head turned quickly in the direction where Ray thought he heard the noise. After a moment of no response, he slid his revolver back into its holster while mumbling to himself, "You're starting to lose your mind, Ray, get your shit together" as he started piling the rocks back onto the grave. Once he stacked up a few of the stones, he went to grab a few more, only to be greeted by a pair of black boots. Ray began looking the figure up and down, noticing that it wore black pants with a trench coat to match it. The trench coat went down to the figure's boots and was torn and tattered at the bottom, flapping wildly in the wind. The figure wore a black, leather cowboy hat that looked like it was composed of bats' wings. Ray fell backward and drew his revolvers. "Don't come any closer, or I will shoot," he warned, aiming at the figure's head. Within seconds, the being drew out its handgun and aimed it at Ray. "Guess peace ain't an option," Ray sarcastically said as he opened fired on the being. Most of the bullets went through the being's chest; however, there was one that went through its head, knocking its hat off in the process. Ray was in a further state of shock than he was previously, as he was introduced to the face of the assailant. The eyes were empty and dark, almost as if it didn't have any, and its entire face had the structure of a skull. "This can't be… "Ray was filled with fear and confusion. *Flashback starts*

When Ray was a kid, his grandmother would tell him many stories. Sometimes those stories were tied back to local myths. One of the myths involved a creature called a soul hunter. Ray always thought that his grandmother Oriella Williams was a very superstitious woman, so when she did share many of the stories with Ray, he would generally take them with a grain of salt. According to his grandmother, Soul Hunters were spiritual creatures whose purpose was to collect the souls of the living and take them to heaven or hell based on how they lived their lives. The beings would be gentle or violent depending on how the human was in their life. These creatures, supposedly, were to guard cemeteries against grave robbers and defilers while not pursuing their prey. According to legend, one would only see these when they are being followed or if the being allows itself to be seen.

Flashback ends The Soul Hunter drew its pistol, which looked like it was composed of some bone fragments. The Skull's jaw started moving as a hiss mixed with the sound of a loud whisper came from its mouth. "For desecrating a grave, you must pay for your sins... The cost is your life. A bolt of blue fire shot from the pistol as Ray rolled out of the line of fire. He then tried to attack the creature again with the birds of prey. Unfortunately, this didn't even seem to phase the hunter. This was when it started to fire back. The bullets shot past Ray, just barely missing him. He was able to roll out of the way, falling back to the ground. The creature re-adjusted the skele-pistol toward Ray's new position, its devious, boney grin seemingly twisting more with each second. The soul hunter then started firing again, which would have gotten Ray if it hadn't been for him rolling toward his left and then sliding behind one of the tombstones near him for cover.

"You might as well stop trying to fight the inevitable," the being hissed. Its eye sockets looked coldly in Ray's direction, and he could feel its malicious intent. Ray realized at this point that there wasn't much he was able to do. So, he decided to try and head toward Old Red and get the hell out of there. "Do you ever need to reload?" Ray yelled. The creature only responded with silence, and the increasing shots fired upon him. Ray proceeded to shuffle from gravestone to gravestone, slowly making progress to where he hitched up Old Red. Looking back for a quick moment, Ray noticed a trail made up of what looked like blue fire following him. After dodging between thirty graves, the cemetery entrance caught Ray's eye. He thought about venturing forward; however, the grave he was behind was taking heavy fire, and there was a significant enough distance between him and the gate with no graves in between. In turn, Ray knew that the lack of cover meant that even the slightest mess up meant he was dead. However, Ray realized that if he didn't move fast enough, this thing would just come around the tombstone he was hiding behind and kill him; he was a sitting duck.

That was when he made a split decision to run for it. "On the count of three, I'm going to bolt for Red and make an escape," Ray thought to himself. "One, two, and…" Ray counted softly to himself as he bolted toward the cemetery gates. With every second increasing, Ray couldn't help but feel that he was getting closer to danger. Finally, he made it to where the cemetery gate meets the desert, only to have something pulled his right leg back as he went to step down. In turn, this caused him to faceplant into the sand. Ray began to cry out in pain due to the immense burning caused by whatever was wrapped around his leg. This caused him to flip on his back and look at what was causing it. The Soul hunter had what looked like a lasso made of the same blue fire that composed the bullets from its gun.

Ray's face evolved into an expression of sheer terror as he was being dragged in like an insect caught in a spider's web. "No, please!" Ray begged for mercy. The skull maintained the malicious grin as the creature kept pulling. Ray unsheathed his hunting knife and threw his body forward, causing himself to sit up. This was when he attempted to grab the rope with his left hand; however, it burned him hotter than hellfire when he tried. Ray's hand jerked back within a matter of seconds, and in turn, caused him to fall to his back again as the creature pulled the lasso violently. Ray held the knife at the ready in preparation for defending his life. The being towered over him at this point, just staring down at him with those dark eye sockets. The

Soul Hunter then drew its bone pistol, aiming it down toward Ray's head, causing him to look up the gun's barrel.

"The other world finds you guilty of grave defilement. Do you have any last words?" the being hissed, its boney finger lay ready on the trigger of the pistol. "Just one." The words came out of his mouth as he swung his knife with all of his might into the being's gun. This caused the creature to loosen its grip and the pistol to soar toward Ray's left. He then used the leverage from the swing to throw his body in the direction of the gun. As he belly-flopped into the sand, he was able to drag himself close enough toward the pistol to snatch it off the ground. Within seconds of picking it up, Ray pointed the gun at the soul hunter's head and then pulled the trigger. A blue hellfire bullet shot the being just between the eyes, causing it to let out an excruciating shriek. The blue fire started to consume every bit of being that the Soul Hunter was as it flailed around, eventually fading into nothing. Ray stood up, slowly letting out a deep sigh that was a combination of exhaustion and relief. He then picked up his knife, sheathed it, and made his way to Old Red at the cemetery gates. Once there, Ray unhitched him, pulled himself onto Old Red's back, and took a moment to look at the detail on the new pistol he obtained. After looking it over for a moment, Ray was puzzled as he couldn't figure out where the gun stored the ammo, what kind it used, or even how many bullets were left. "I best use this only in situations where nothing else is working," Ray thought to himself as he slipped the pistol into one of his duster coat's pockets. Ray then grabbed Old Red's reins and navigated him back to his home to get some rest and prepare for what tomorrow had planned.

Chapter 7 Home Planning, Home Sick, Home Field Advantage

Ray's Homestead was located northwest of Maple. As soon as the duo made it, Ray slid off of Old Red and then led him into the small stable where he used to keep Smokey when he wasn't riding him. "This ain't yours, but we will figure out something a little more permanent with time." Ray ensured his new steed. After Ray secured Old Red in the stable, he headed out of the building and into his home. His house was a three-bedroom, two-story building which looked like it was assembled with the same kind of wood that most of Maple was. The house had a massive wooden porch wrapped around it, and there was only one set of stairs composed of three steps that led onto the platform. As Ray walked in the door, he followed the hallway to the stairs and made his way up to the second floor. He began removing multiple articles of clothing as he entered the room to the right, at the top of the stairwell. He then laid them on top of one of the dressers and forced up the energy to make it into bed. Within minutes of his head hitting the pillow, Ray fell asleep.

The sunlight radiated through a window that faced the east, filling up the room like water in a glass that was just topped off. Ray rolled over to his left to see Elaine sleeping next to him. The sun reflected off of each strand of her gorgeous golden hair, and she had that slight grin that she had most mornings when she was comfortable and happy. "Good Morning, Beautiful." Ray whispered in her ear with a softness to his tone that Elaine hadn't heard in years. Her eyes slowly opened, revealing the baby blue eyes that he found himself lost in time and time again. "Well, good morning to you, Mr. Williams." Elaine responded, her voice as soft as ever. Ray started running his fingers through the blonde strands of hair on the bed. "With you by my side, I cannot help but sleep well, Mr. Williams." The words softly came out of her mouth.

   Ray pulled himself up from the bed and proceeded to get ready for the day. The final article of clothing that he had to put on was his shirt, which, as soon as he buttoned up the top button, the room became consumed in darkness. Ray looked out the window to see an ocean of stars. "Damn, this is weird." he whispered to himself, as an intense coughing sound came from where Elaine lay. Ray's attention shifted toward the dark outline of his beloved, which was now violently shaking in conjunction with the coughs. After a few minutes, her body became limp and void of all movement. Ray bolted around to her side of the bed, rushing to make sure she was okay. Even next to Elaine, Ray could still only make out the outline of her body for a moment. Slowly, his eyes became more accustomed to the dark, and he could see her in more detail.

    The sight completely caught Ray off guard as he fell back in terror. His beloved Elaine's eyes were sunk into the point where they looked like empty eye cavities; her lips looked as if maggots ate at them, and they almost decayed to the point of non-existence. Elaine's long, beautiful gold locks of hair were no longer gold but a pale grey color. The length became a mix of a few long strands and a few short ones. His beloved slowly raised her body from the bed; her chest led the way as her head and arms continued to dangle almost as if they were devoid of life. Elaine's head violently jerked forward with her body in an upright position until it was in its original place. What little hair she had left covered her face as she slowly turned her head toward Ray, pausing once her empty eye sockets were pointing in his direction. "Your time is coming, Mr. Williams." Her voice contained the same familiar ring that it constantly had; the only difference was that she now had a bit of a hiss included.

"What do you mean?" Ray asked; his voice was trembling at this point. Elaine pulled herself out of bed and slowly trod across the hardwood floor as she continued answering Ray. "You are not long for the world of the living." Ray's face became pale, and the hair stood up on the back of his neck. "So I am dy-dy- dying?" Elaine was to the point where she loomed over Ray. "Yes, however..." She lunged at Ray wrapping her boney, decaying, right claw around his neck. She then utilized the momentum from her position to pin him to the ground. "You're not long for the world of the dead either, Mr. Williams." Elaine's body became still for a moment, and Ray could not take his eyes off of her empty cavities. Her jaw jerked violently open, letting out a cracking noise almost as if it were fighting through rigor mortis, and then without even so much warning, she started to regurgitate gallons of warm blood all over Ray's face. Ray tried to fight back by pulling her arms away from his neck. However, Elaine's grip was too firm and just wouldn't budge. The blood filled his lungs through his nose and eventually his mouth when he tried to yell for Elaine to stop. There was a tightness in his chest as he attempted to gasp for air. Just before everything went black, Elaine stopped vomiting the blood. She started to smile as much as she could through the decayed lips while saying, "I love you, Mr. Williams."

Ray shot up from bed and sweat dripped down his face while he hyperventilated. The sun just started peaking through the window, notifying him that morning had finally arrived. Looking around, he was hoping Elaine would be there in the way she had been any other time he woke from a nightmare. Alas, her warm embrace was no were to be found. After a moment of taking everything in, Ray pulled himself out of bed, making his way to where he placed his clothes. Once fully dressed, he made his way down to the kitchen and started up some coffee. Ray then pulled out one of the chairs from his table and took a seat. "Okay, so I know for a fact this Fowler guy ain't dead, or at least his body ain't in its grave." He took his hat off for a moment, running his fingers through his hair as he analyzed the situation. "I probably should make my way over to sheriff Johnson's Office and explain to him what the hell is going on."

The coffee pot whistled, informing Ray that morning brew was ready for consumption. He then slid his chair away from the table, stood up and made his way over to the stove, and finally poured himself the cup of coffee into one of the little white coffee cups that he kept next to that area. After two sips of coffee, Ray's face cringed out of disgust. This threw him off as he always loved the flavor of a hot cup of joe. His stomach was turning, and he felt as if another sip would cause him to vomit. So, without a second thought, he took his cup to the sink and poured it down the drain. Placing his cup on the counter, he headed out toward the stable to ready up Old Red. With both Ray and his steed prepared, the two of them headed back into town to reconnect with the good sheriff.

Chapter 8 Old and New Friends

After around a fifteen-minute ride, Ray slid off his horse and hitched it to the same post that Smokey was tied to last time they stopped by the sheriff's office. Once he was secured, Ray then walked up the old familiar stairs and through the door into the sheriff's office. His eyes quickly adjusted to see the sheriff leaning back in his chair, both of his dust-covered cowboy boots on the desk. "Well, well, well, look at what the cat dragged in." the sheriff said, poking fun at him. "For a moment there, I thought I was going to have to send someone to find you." Ray chuckled. "Very funny, but save your comedy for someone else, you clown bastard." he joked, getting a laugh out of the sheriff. "So Ray, to what do I owe this pleasure?" Ray took a deep breath, "It's that case that I took, trying to locate O'Brian's daughter. I am at a crossroads at the moment." Ray removed the pocket watch from his satchel, tossing it toward the sheriff. He caught it, opening up the lid to examine it while asking, "A pocket watch?"

Ray started to explain the situation. "I tracked the outlaws to the mineshaft located in Red Rock Canyon. I made it deep into the tunnels to find O'Brian's daughter hanging by a lantern hook only to have one of those shifty outlaw bastards jump on my back and bite me." The sheriff dropped his feet off the desk; his face became as serious as a heart attack. "This, in turn, caused me to pass out; heaven only knows for how long. After regaining my consciousness, I started to make my way back toward the entrance, finding this on the ground." The sheriff intently listened as he rubbed his fingers over his chin. "Go on." Ray nodded as he continued. "After doing some investigating, I discovered that this watch," he said, pulling the watch out and holding it in his open palm, "belonged to some guy named Travis Anthony Fowler. The odd thing is, supposedly he died and was buried with it."

The sheriff interrupted with concern in his voice. "You didn't start robbing graves, did you?" Ray became agitated. "No damn it, I done told you where I got the watch! Anyway, long story short, I investigated his grave and noticed the dirt and the rocks that covered it were loose compared to the surrounding ones. Sherriff, I don't think this guy is dead." The sheriff had an annoyed look spread across his face as his eyebrows raised. "You're out of your damn mind if you think there is a dead guy out there walking around." his voice was raised while pointing his finger toward himself. "I ain't no damn coroner, but the way I understand it is once you're dead, you are dead. There is no coming back, there is no walking around, and they're sure as hell ain't no abducting girls." Ray scuffed and started to walk toward the door as a mild coughing fit started up. Noticing Ray was struggling to catch his breath, the sheriff asked if he was ok. "Don't worry about it. I'll be just fine," Ray quietly stated as he walked outside, the doors swinging in his trail.

    As Ray proceeded to walk down the steps, a voice caught him off guard, saying, "I believe you." Ray turned around to see a man leaning against the wall of the sheriff's office. The man looked as if he were in his early thirties. His face was so tan it almost looked as if it were bronze, and his attire was composed of tan jeans and a button-up shirt of the same color. Over the tan shirt, the man wore a leather duster which was just a slightly darker shade, and the color of his boots matched. The man's eyes were a dark brown and had slight bags under them indicating being tired and also told a silent tale of his experience. One of the features that stood out was a scar in the shape of a claw that went from his left eyebrow to the top part of his left cheek.

Ray's voice became stern. "Were you eavesdropping?" The man responded, "So what if was?" He queried Ray with a little bit of a snarl to his smile. "We might have a problem then, friend." The man utilized his foot to push himself off of the wall. "Relax, I'm not here to hurt you. If I were, you would already be dead." Ray raised his eyebrows as he interrupted, "You're so sure about that?" The man answered so quickly he almost cut him off. "Based on your limp and the fact that you seem kind of pale, yeah, I would say it's a safe bet." The man continued, then reaching his hand out offering a handshake. Ray just looked at it, then shifted his eye back toward the man's staring. "Who the hell are you?" The man kept his hand up as an offering. "The name's Mavrick, Mavrick O'Connell."

Ray didn't even budge, only offering his cold stare back, with his response matching it. "What do you want?" Mavrick continued from before. "As I told you before, I believe what you're saying. I also don't think the man you are looking for is a man at all." Ray interrogated him. "What do you mean?" Finally giving up on the handshake, Mavrick let his hand fall to the side. "Well, when it comes to the world, we only see a small portion of what there is; case in point, look at what happened with your friend there. What was his name, Fowler?" Ray snapped, "Don't be cute! He ain't my friend!" Mavrick placed his hands up in surrender. "Didn't mean nothing by it. Anyway, I had seen this sort of thing before. I used to know a man named Winston. He was a good man. Winston used to be a regular patron at a bar I frequently visited. The last time I talked with him, he had a slight cough and was pale. Sure enough, the next time I went to the establishment, the barkeep told me that he passed away." Mavrick slowly lowered his hands to his side again.

"After breaking the news, he told me that they buried him out on the outskirts of the town. Naturally, after finishing up my bourbon, I proceeded to make my way over there to pay my respects." Ray asked, "Okay, so how does this relate to Fowler?" Mavrick looked annoyed, ignoring the question. He continued with his recollection. "I made it to the grave around dusk after searching for a while. I noticed the dirt and stones that covered his grave seemed to be moving." Ray's eyes opened wide as ever. "Moving?" Mavrick continued nodding, "Yep, you heard me right. I knelt closer to the grave to ensure my eyes weren't playing tricks on me, and a hand shot out of the ground. Completely caught off guard, I fell onto my back, and I couldn't help but just sit there and watch as my old friend dug himself out of his own grave. Once completely free of the dirt and stones, Winston laid there for a moment as I quickly rose to my feet. I asked twice if he was okay as I tread slowly toward him, and the only response I got was silence. Finally, being next to him, I knelt to one of my knees to attempt to get close enough to feel a pulse. Without even a moment's notice, he lunged up, wrapping his cold hands around my throat, causing me to fall on my back as he was choking me. I wedged my hands in between his grip and my throat and did everything I could think of to loosen up his grip, but nothing seemed to work." Mavrick looked down at his boots, concealing his face behind his hat. "Winston's face still looked as it did from when he was alive except for his eyes. They were the same color and all, but he just had a mad look in him. His grip was so strong, the only thing that I was able to do was to take my knife out and stab that poor bastard in the head until he let go, screamed, and ran off in the other direction."

Ray's tone softened a bit at this point. "That is awful." he said, his face displaying a disgusted look. "Sure is." Mavrick agreed as he nodded his head. Gunfire started going off in the local bank, catching Ray and Mavrick's attention. Ray unhitched Old Red, and both men unhitched their horses and bolted toward their next destination. Once there, they saw three men walking out. All of them were wearing black suits, which looked in pristine condition, and red bandanas on their faces to conceal their identity. The guy in the middle raised his silver pistol into the air and shot off a round while shouting, "Alright boys, you know the drill!" The two other outlaws then started loading up a charcoal-colored carriage with an abundance of bags from the bank.

      Ray took a few steps closer and raised his voice enough to ensure they could hear him. "What the hell do you think you're doing?" he pulled his duster to the side, revealing both of the handles of his Birds of Prey. The three outlaws instantly stopped and drew their attention toward Ray. The middle guy began to lash out. "What did you say, boy?" Ray's eyes met his, almost as if he were trying to stare him down. "Do I have to spell it out for you?" He repeated himself slowly. "What the hell do you think you're doing?" The guy in the middle started laughing so hard he was almost howling. "You see this, boys? This damn crip thinks he can stop us." Both of the men behind him accompanied him in laughter. "If you think you're so tough that you can handle a cripple, why don't you take me on one by one. No friends, no tricks, just the two of us." Ray said.

His hands never once left the sides of his revolvers. The guy in the center's laughter continued. "Okay, it's your funeral. Boys, why don't you enjoy your break. After all, it's going to be a short one."

    Ray proceeded to make his way out to the middle of the dusty road as the outlaw's leader matched him. Anyone in earshot of the challenge cleared the streets and went into the entryways of buildings. For those who hadn't picked up on it, they joined them quickly. "Count of ten, then fire?" Ray confirmed. The outlaw nodded in agreeance. "One, two, three" both men started counting. "four, five, six." The outlaw placed his right hand on the brown handle of his pistol, and Ray's eyes followed it, observing every slight twitch that his hand made as a form of insurance. "seven, eight, nine, ten." As the outlaw drew his pistol, Ray did the same with both of his Birds of Prey revolvers. The Outlaw managed to get the barrel pointing toward Ray's head, but before he could get a shot off, Ray beat him to it, firing his right revolver first and then his left. The first bullet ricocheted off of where the muzzle and the revolver barrel met, causing the outlaw to loosen his grip and the gun to fly off to the right. The bullet from the left revolver wasn't as kind, shooting directly in between the eyes of the outlaw, causing dust to rise around his corpse to hit the ground with a loud thud. Immediately both of the other outlaws drew their guns on Ray, only to abruptly fall backward in a similar fashion to their leader, not even having time to scream as they hit the ground. Ray looked around in a state of shock as he thought he was dead. He didn't even have a moment to cock his revolver. The sound of someone blowing down the muzzle of the gun came from behind him. As he turned around, he saw Mavrick sliding his two firearms into their holsters as a grin came across his face, and he said, "You're welcome."

     Mavrick started pacing back and forth in front of Ray. "So, as I was saying before, I may be able to be of assistance." Ray acknowledged this while still dealing with the revelation that if it weren't for Mavrick being there, he might have been pushing up daisies. "Okay, Mavrick, I am listening. How can you help me?" Mavrick stopped pacing, turning his complete focus toward Ray. "Well, for one, I'm a hell of a shot. You won't ever be in a situation where you're outgunned." Ray nodded as he continued trying to figure him out. "So why do you want to help me?" Mavrick's sincerity flowed from his voice like water from a river. "Honestly, there is just too much evil in the world. Too much stuff that kills people, tears families apart, and leaves kids in broken homes." He paused for a moment and sighed. "I was a victim of this myself, and I just don't want anyone else to suffer the way I did."

Mavrick then took a deep breath and shook his head, clearing his slightly disturbed expression from his face. "Anyway, I didn't mean to be rude and listen in on your conversation with the sheriff." Ray had a mildly irritated look on his face once again. "Right, why did you do that again?" Mavrick continued. "Honestly, what caught my ear was you two talking about Red Rock Canyon. I was camping out around the outskirts of the canyon right around the same time that you dealt with those outlaws. I just remember it was dark, and while sitting around the campfire, I heard a bunch of horses galloping out from the canyon. Based on the sound of the direction that the horse's gallops disappeared into the night, I would say that it is safe that they were headed southwest toward Saint Edgerton." Ray attentively stared while Mavrick resumed. "Once again, friend, I didn't mean anything by listening in, hell I would have turned a blind ear if I didn't think I could help."

Ray put his index finger up for a moment to stop interrupting Mavrick. "Saint Edgerton, ain't that roughly a two-day trip?" Mavrick responded, "Normally, as long as you don't run into anything to slow you down." Ray interrupted. "Ok, let's go." He turned around, walking toward Old Red, getting ready for their journey. Mavrick pulled himself onto his horse, saying "Meet me in front of the general store when you are ready to head out. We should stock up on supplies to help ensure our trip is trouble-free." Ray nodded, and both men made their way to the general store. They went inside for a moment to stock up, and then the two of them headed out to Saint Edgerton, leaving nothing but a trail of dust behind.

Chapter 9 Not Out of the Woods Just Yet

The time rode by quickly; seconds turned into minutes and those into hours. The terrain slowly morphed, transforming from the old sandy desert to beautiful green pastures. Inevitably the sun began setting, encouraging both Ray and Mavrick to set up camp for the night. Eventually, they found the perfect spot, the top of the large hill. What made this spot so good from their point of view was that the sides were surrounded by woods making it more difficult to spot them. Along with this, the terrain was flat, making it the perfect spot to set up the fire and get some rest.

Both men found a tree with a sturdy trunk and lined their horses up to it, and they slid off the horses. Both men then took the reins tying them around the tree, ensuring that they wouldn't run off in the night. Ray then made his way to the back end of the horse, grabbing the bedroll that was stowed on him while Mavrick did the same thing with his horse. Each of the men rolled out their sleeping bags along the outskirts of where they planned to set up their fire. "Ok, one of us needs to go find some firewood for the camp fi-"(Ray started having another coughing fit) Mavrick walked over to Ray, placing his hand on his shoulder. "Are you

Ok?" After a moment, he regained his breath and his composure. Ray reassured him that he was fine. "Either way, go rest up. I will go and find some firewood." Mavrick started making his way into the woods surrounding them while Ray stumbled over to his sleeping bag. Once he was semi-comfortable, Ray removed his hat, placed it on his chest, and dozed off.

  Moments later, Ray shot out of his sleep to the sound of a loud howling coming from within the woods. Ray's eyes dashed, trying to pinpoint the location of the noise. With no cloud in sight, the entire area was completely lit up by the stars and the full moon, making everything easy to see. Ray had a look on his face of pure exhaustion. "What now?" he muttered to himself. He then walked over to Mavrick's sleeping bag, whispering loudly in an attempt to wake him, but to no avail. Not only was Mavrick's sleeping bag empty, but there wasn't even a piece of wood or an ash spot in the ground where he expected the fire to be. "Shit, whatever that was, it must have got Mavrick!" Ray started to try and figure out what to do. Another howl filled the brisk air, a little bit louder than the previous one. Ray forced himself up and made his way to the center of the hill. Once there, he drew the Birds of Prey from their holsters, cocking them as a non-verbal warning that he wasn't in a mood to be trifled with.

    The trees in front of him started shaking violently, and Ray could hear a faint growl from amongst them. He pulled both peacemakers to the ready and yelled "You want a piece of me?! Come get some!" The immense creature crawled out of the woods with a massive snarl smeared across its face. The monster was covered with an overabundance of black fur, and the claws were even darker. The creature looked like a wolf but was larger than Ray had ever seen before. It then opened its massive jaw, revealing a ton of sharp fangs and releasing a roar that thundered through the air. Without even a moment's hesitation, Ray started open firing. The being fell on all fours, rushing Ray faster than a bull that saw red and rammed him with the top of its head, knocking him to his back. With the creature looming over him at this point, Ray instinctively took a few more shots with the Birds of Prey. Those shots were in vain as all it seemed to do was piss the monster off.

    The monster's snarl widened, looking as if it was about to take a bite. Without thinking, Ray dropped the revolver in his right hand and unsheathed his knife, thrusting it into the left eye of the creature. The being stumbled back, releasing a blood-curdling howl, causing Ray to drop his weapons and cover his ears. The beast flailed around in pain and quickly ran off into the woods. Ray promptly pulled himself off the ground, snatching up all his weapons and placing them in their proper holsters. "I may have scared him off, but I have a feeling that it will be back." Ray whispered to himself as he was looking around in an attempt to plan out his next move. His first thought was to stay where he was and wait for Mavrick to reappear; however, he figured it had to have been a couple of hours based on where the moon was in the sky. After mulling it over a bit, Ray figured that due to the time that had passed along with how resilient the creature was, there was little chance that Mavrick would be able to survive an encounter with it.

    Without a second thought, Ray made his way over to Mavrick's horse, taking a lasso hanging on the saddlebag and swiftly hanging it around its neck. While doing this, he was consistently whispering to it, reassuring it that everything would be ok. The woods directly behind Ray started rustling as if a storm was beginning to brew, and even though the leaves and branches were loud, the growl that projected from within them was far noisier. Ray sprinted to Old Red, pulling himself onto the saddle while never loosening his tight grip on the lasso. The monster lunged out of the woods and landed mere inches away from the sleeping bags still lying on the ground. Ray yelled out a "Hyyyahh!!!" as he drove his spurs into the sides of his steed, causing it to let out a loud squeal and stormed off in a gallop.

    Old Red started dodging trees while Mavrick's horse followed close behind. Ray looked back for a moment, and it looked like the wolf wasn't having a problem keeping up with them as it was right on the tail of Mavrick's horse. Mavrick took his right hand off Old Red's reins and pulled his right birds of prey revolver out of its holster. While doing this, he tightened his grip with his legs in the hope that he wouldn't get pulled or fall off in his attempt to keep a tight grip on the lasso and maintain his balance. Aiming toward the beast, Ray adjusted his shot, pointing it closer to the creature's face. "This thing's eye seems to be its weakness. If I hit it just right, I may be able to slow this thing down a bit." he whispered to himself as he inhaled deeply. While exhaling all of the air that filled his lungs, he closed his left eye and exploited his right one to get the most accurate shot. Ray then pulled the trigger, firing his revolver. However, Old Red jerked to the right at the last moment, causing him to shake the gun, clipping the wolf in its ear.

    The creature let out a sharp yip but suffered no loss of its momentum. Ray then cocked back the hammer of his revolver in preparation to take another shot. Before he could let off another round, however, the beast pounced forward, sinking its claws into Mavrick's steed's hindquarters. The wolf dragged it to the ground violently, and in turn, forced Ray to lose his grip on the lasso. In an attempt to save the life of the poor steed Ray took a few more shots with his revolver. The severity of the situation seemed to be taking hold as only one bullet hit him, nicking the monster in the neck. The creature's growl became more feral for a moment as the creature looked up and opened its wide mouth, exposing its sharp razor blade-like fangs. Sadly, the shot delayed the inevitable as both the wolf and the horse became entirely consumed by the darkness and trees. Ray heard a whining sound followed by the sound of flesh ripping and bones crunching. Due to dropping the lasso and no longer being held back by the other horse, Old Red was able to pick up more speed on its gallop, in turn causing Ray to slip the gun back into its holster and turn his attention around toward the path. Sure of the horse's demise, Ray figured the only thing to do now was utilize the beast's distraction to gain as much ground as quickly as possible.

    Ray and Old Red continued going hard until they saw the woods opening that led out into open pastures. The moon began to hide among the horizon while Ray pulled the pocket watch out, giving it a moment to adjust. He could see that the second hand pointed to the five o'clock position. This indicated to Ray that he was headed southwest. Ray let out a breath of relief, grateful that he had maintained his course even amongst all the madness. Exhaustion started to take its toll on Ray, and his cough progressed even more violently than previous ones. He eventually stumbled across a tree with a relatively small trunk compared to the ones he dodged most of the night. Once Old Red was mere inches away from the tree, Ray freed his feet from the stirrup, dropped to the ground, led the horse by its reins, and tied the draw around the base of the trunk. Ray then made his way to the other side of the tree, leaning his back against it and sliding down until he was sitting in mud. Ray's head tilted forward, and he started dozing off, losing consciousness once again.

Ray was greeted by the pale ceiling staring back at him as his eyes opened. The sun radiated as bright as ever, filling the room much like water fills a lake. He rolled over to his right and saw his beloved Elaine's blonde hair covering most of the pillow next to him. Ray then leveraged his weight to roll himself back in the opposite direction until he was able to thrust his legs toward the edge of the bed. With his feet making contact with the hardwood floor, he pushed his hands against the mattress to assist him to his feet. Ray then strolled over to the dresser and rummaged through in preparation for facing the day.

Instantly the room became un-illuminated, and the atmosphere triggered something in Ray, causing him to realize that he had been in this situation before. "Shit!" he whispered sort of loudly to himself, as against his better judgment, he turned toward the bed to see a dark figure standing over it. For a moment, he thought it may have been Elaine until he recognized her faint outline lying in bed. "Who the hell are you!" Ray yelled as the figure's dark face allowed a sinister smile to come across it, exposing two sharp fangs. The creature disregarded Ray's demand as it crouched down where Elaine was resting. "Get away from her, you son of a bitch!" Ray yelled as he rushed toward the being. Before he could make it around the end of the bed, the figure vanished, and his eyes shifted over to where his beloved laid.

Beams of moonlight flowed through the window, illuminating Elaine's face. Her eyes slowly opened as she smiled at Ray. "What's wrong, Mr. Williams?" she asked with the sweet sincerity that Ray only knew from her. A tear slipped out from his right tear duct while he smiled, making it clear that he was undergoing an emotional war. "Nothing, sweetheart, I just am so happy to see you again." Elaine then asked him, "So when are you going to do it?" A look of confusion made its way across Ray's already complicated face. "I'm sorry?" Ray added the look of confusion to his already complex facial expressions. Elaine started to laugh the soft laugh that she always had before; no matter the situation, this always had a way of putting Ray at ease. "Kiss me, you silly man." After a slight hesitation, he obliged, leaning in for a kiss. He placed his left hand under her head and his right behind her back, pulling her in, and their lips met. Ray couldn't help but close his eyes, lost in the moment.

Once he opened his eyes, he was staring into the empty eye sockets of the woman he once loved. Completely caught off guard Ray pushed himself away and stumbled backward, falling to the ground. "Oh my god!" Ray yelled in terror as the withered corpse, a former shadow of his beloved, started crawling out of bed. The slow jerking movements couldn't help but remind one of a spider's legs after being crushed. While Elaine sauntered her way over to Ray, he aggressively shuffled backward in an attempt to avoid being within the grappling range of his beloved. Unfortunately for him, he only had so far that he could go before the wall stopped him. Elaine continued until she was looming over him. "Elaine, please no, stop!" Ray's voice shook more than a leaf in fall on a windy day. "What's wrong, Mr. Williams ain't you happy to see me?" What was left of her lips attempted to form a smile.

"This can't be real; you can't be. This isn't possible!" Ray responded, ignoring the question. Elaine then reached one of her putrefied hands toward Ray, placed it on his shoulder, and knelt next to him. "I have something I need to tell you, Mr. Williams." The look of sheer terror mixed with disgust was plastered across his face as he couldn't stop staring at her mouth and how it looked like she was chewing anytime that she was talking due to the lack of lips. "You don't long for the world of the living." Ray's eyes somehow managed to become even more open than before. "What...what do you mean?" his voice shuddered softly, showing how much terror he had. Some of the muscles on her face started to tense up, causing the decaying smile to look even more malicious than before as she swiftly transitioned her hand from his shoulder to his throat. "You know what I mean, Mr. Williams." The words came from her mouth almost as a hiss as she repositioned her face directly in front of Ray's. "However, you are also not long for the world of the dead either."

  Ray shot up out of his sleep screaming, only to see the outline of a man standing over him with the barrel of a gun pointing toward his face. Even though it was hard to see due to the sun being directly behind the man, Ray's eyes adjusted enough to where he was barely able to make out the figure. "Mavrick, you're o-?" Mavrick intervened swiftly, with a bit of a growl in his voice. "Of course, why wouldn't I be? It ain't as you left me for dead." Ray could hear the sarcasm at the root of every word that fell out of his mouth. "Mavrick, I swear, I thought you were dead." Ray raised his hands, showing Mavrick that he wasn't looking for a fight.

"Well, clearly I wasn't. Now, do you mind telling me where the hell my horse and supplies are?" Ray stared directly into his eyes " Well, Mavrick, what happened is when you went into the woods, I ended up dozing off. After waking up a few hours later, I realized that there were no traces of the firewood that you went to get. Next thing that I knew, a giant wolf flew out of the woods and attacked me." Mavrick smirked and nodded his head in disbelief toward the side. "Ok, now I suppose that you are going to tell me that the wolf thing killed my horse and destroyed all of my supplies?" Ray let out a sigh as he nodded slowly. "I took the rope off your horse's saddle, lassoing it around its neck. I thought I was going to prevent it from being mauled by that creature while trying to save some of the supplies, but I was unable to do so."

Ray then took notice of something that he had not prior. Mavrick's right eye seemed to have a scarred look that wasn't there prior. "There's no way!" Ray thought to himself while attempting to rationalize another potential explanation on how this could be. "What happened to your eye?" Ray asked sternly. Mavrick stopped him. "Finish your story first, and then I will tell you mine." knowing it was the

84

only way to get Mavrick to cooperate, Ray picked from where he left off.

"As I was saying, the wolf attacked us, and I attempted to hold it off, but it overpowered me. That was when I made the call to move out. Like I said prior, that monster didn't give me a lot of time to grab much. I could only get a hold of your horse before that thing lunged at us. Thankfully the wolf missed your horse and me, giving us enough time to take off into the woods. Unfortunately, we could not maintain a speed fast enough to lose it. Without a moment's notice, it lunged out of the darkness, latching on to the hindquarters of your horse. After a moment of fighting the wolf, kicking and flailing around, it finally succumbed to the weight of the beast, stumbling to the ground as the rope I was holding slid out of my hands following it. Rather than just riding away, I even attempted to shoot the wolf a few times only to miss." Ray pointed at his horse. "Old Red here was startled and wouldn't slow down for some time, no matter what I did. It had to be near dawn by the time we finally reached where we are now, and due to the exhaustion, we had to rest." Ray started glaring at Mavrick. "Okay, now the eye, what happened? Spit it out."

Mavrick's stance changed from an aggressive one to a much more relaxed one. "Honestly, I have no idea," he recalled proceeding to lower his revolver. "All I know is I went into the woods, looking for the firewood, and I ended up getting lost. While wandering around aimlessly, the moon made its way above the roof of the woods, illuminating a small path for me. I then remember looking up at the moon and thinking how beautiful it looked that night." Mavrick slipped his revolver into its holster while continuing his recollection. "Then the world just went dark. Honestly, I thought I had just fallen asleep, but when I woke up, I noticed my sight in my right eye seemed a little cloudy, and all my clothes had been shredded. Thankfully I stumbled across some of my clothes as I was attempting to make my way out of those damn woods." Mavrick then reached out a hand to Ray, offering his assistance in getting up.

Ray hesitated for a moment, wondering if Mavrick could be a monster and be completely unaware of it. After shaking off his hesitation, Ray grabbed Mavrick's hand, and he pulled himself off of the ground. Once he was upright and Ray planted both feet firmly against the ground, he made his way over to Old Red and unhitched him while

Mavrick pulled himself onto his horse. Ray looked up at Mavrick with a confused and slightly frustrated look on his face, "Just what in the hell do you think you are doing?" Mavrick smirked and pulled his hat down to cover his eyes from the sun, "Oh, you know, just riding shotgun." Ray shook his head slightly in disapproval while making his way over to his horse. "Why should I let you do that?" Ray interrogated Mavrick. "Well, for one, I still plan on helping you to track down those out," Ray couldn't help but interrupt Mavrick with yet another coughing fit. "Another reason is that coughing makes you sound like you're knocking at death's door and making more friends right now is probably in your best interest." Ray released a loud sigh out of exhaustion. "Fine, let's just get a move on it." Ray pulled himself up on the main part of the saddle and turned Old Red's head toward the southwest. Ray then let out a "Hiyaa" as he pulled the lead up and whipped it down gently while tapping the sides of Old Red with his spurs. All three of them continued forward and made their way down to Saint Edgerton.

Chapter 10 Welcome to Saint Edgerton

After traveling most of the day, a welcome sign greeted the men with a sign displaying *"Welcome to Saint Edgerton."* This area was scorching, similar to the climate that Ray grew up in, but unlike there, this climate was far more humid. Neither of the men was surprised by this because swamps had surrounded them for the last two hours. In turn, neither of them expected it to cause Ray to have a more challenging time with his breathing, which was evident in his slight shortness of breath.

Saint Edgerton was a town that was like no other. The streets were made of brick except for a few alleys, and most of the buildings were two to three stories high. Along with this, most of them had a spear-like symbol that seemed to be engraved on every other building. Most of the homes had black as coal gates that looked like they were made of cast iron. The top of the gates either had spikes or the spear-like symbol found on most surrounding buildings.

After making it through the city, a general goods store caught Mavrick's eye down at the tail end of the long road. Pointing it out to Ray, he then requested that they stop off so that he may be able to pick up some more supplies. Ray obliged, "That's fine. I should run in and grab a few things as well." Ray then slowed his horse down to a stop, slid off it, and hitched it to one of the many hitching posts outside the shop. With Old Red secured, Mavrick made his way off the horse, and both men headed into the shop.

As the door opened, a small bell rang, alerting the shopkeep that he had company. "Welcome folks. How can I be of assistance?" Ray chimed in, "Well, we are looking to stock up on some supplies." Ray made his way over to a set of wooden shelves that held a variety of canned and jarred food goods. "Not a problem. If you have any questions, let me know. " Ray continued making his way through the canned goods while Mavrick headed up to the counter. "Yeah mister, I have a question. Where can I find some clothing?" The shopkeeper just pointed through a door open in the store's back corner. Mavrick then nodded his hat and walked through the door, disappearing into the back room.

Two men dressed in black, except the red bandanas, walked into the store within seconds. One of them pulled out a pistol concealed under a trench coat and aimed down the sights on the shopkeep. He then yelled in a deep voice "Put your hands up! This is a fucking robbery!" The other guy quickly ran over to Ray and placed his gun on his back. "Don't even think about turning around!" The second outlaw yelled at Ray as he complied and raised his hands to the sky, showing he wasn't a threat. His voice quivered a little bit. "There ain't no need to be hast-" The second outlaw interrupted, "You keep talking, and I will shoot you dead!" Simultaneously, the first outlaw pulled out a tan sack, which looked stained by dirt or dust on the outside. He removed it from the inner lining of his duster. He forced it into the hands of the shopkeep while growling at him. "If you know what is good for you, you will fill this bag to the brim with all your cash, starting with the register."

    Mavrick silently came out the doorway, holding his revolvers to the ready, aiming at each one of the outlaw's heads. Mavrick cleared his throat then yelled at the outlaws. "You best put your guns down before I turn both of your brains into swiss cheese!" The second outlaw looked at the first one, and uncertainty filled what little one could see of his eyes. The first one looked back at the second one for a moment. The fire in his eyes was flaring, and he was mad. "No problem, mister. We don't want no trouble." The first outlaw said the sarcasm poured out of him like a waterfall.

Without any notice, he then turned around while dropping to the ground and firing off a round in Mavrick's direction. Based on the shot's trajectory, it would have killed Mavrick if it weren't for him slightly tilting his head to the right. This caused it to whiz past his ear as Mavrick fired a shot from his revolver. This bullet caused the first outlaw's head to whip backward, followed by a pool of blood that started to seep out from the wound.

"Are you going to try anything funny, sweetheart?" Mavrick asked, raising the other revolver back up as if getting ready to shoot him. The outlaw's voice shook more than a leaf on a tree in midfall. "N-no." Mavrick then continued. "Good, then drop your gun and put your hands in the air, like the good little bitch you are." The outlaw dropped the gun, and his hands went up slowly; his facial expression displayed that he knew he was in a bad situation. Once he heard the gun hit the ground, Ray turned around, cocked his fist back, and slugged the outlaw in the face. The outlaw hit the ground like a sack of bricks. Shaking his hand, Ray then looked toward the shopkeep. "You by chance have any rope?" Ray asked. "My partner and I had some, but unfortunately, it got destroyed." The man nodded yes in response as he made his way to the backroom. A moment later, came out holding two separated hundred-foot ropes, each in its own arm. The shopkeep then made his way over to Mavrick, handing him one of the ropes and then over to Ray, doing the same. Not wasting any time, Ray used it to tie up the outlaw's hands while thanking the shopkeep. He then lifted the crook off the hardwood floor to his feet. He then placed his right hand on the right shoulder of the outlaw's duster jacket while grabbing ahold of the outlaw's arm with his left just in case he tried anything funny.

 Mavrick then made his way over to the store's main register with an eye patch as black as midnight and placed it on the counter. He then asked, "How much for the eye patch, friend?" The shopkeeper ran his fingers across his chin. "Normally, I would charge seventy-one cents, but you two saved me a lot of headache and money by taking care of these two trouble makers. Please take it as a token of my gratitude." Mavrick then reached his right hand out, meeting with the shopkeepers. The two men embraced in a handshake. Ray chimed in. "Don't worry about this half-wit; we will take care of him." The shopkeeper nodded his head. "Perfect. I will take care of the authorities if y'all need to head out." They exchanged thanks once again, then Mavrick, Ray, and the outlaw made their way to Old Red.

Taking off his hat, Mavrick slipped the eyepatch over his eye and repositioned his hat as he walked over to where Ray was standing. Mavrick then grabbed the outlaw on the shoulder so that Ray could unhitch the horse and ride it. "You sure you got him?" Ray asked. Mavrick smirked a little as a small chuckle escaped his mouth Mavrick continued pointing at the outlaw. "Oh, I think I can handle this dumb bastard. Besides, if numbnuts here tries anything funny, I feel that I may have a better chance of getting him under control." The outlaw looked down at his boots as he mumbled under his breath and shook his head, and Mavrick taunted him. "Ain't that right numbnuts?" Ray threw his arm up, covering his mouth as he started to have a coughing fit. "Fine." Ray managed to force the word out between deep gasps of breaths while releasing his tight grip off of the outlaw.

Mavrick took one of his revolvers out and placed the muzzle of the gun against the outlaw's back. Mavrick turned his body enough so that the outlaw could look him dead in the eyes. "Mind you, boy, I would strongly recommend against trying anything funny." The severe look grew into a smirk, "Or not, I ain't had target practice in a hot second."

The outlaw's eyes told a concerning tale. Ray then made his way over to where his horse was hitched, released it, and pulled himself onto his horse's saddle. Mavrick then asked Ray "Do you have any good ideas on where we can take this guy for a moment, maybe ask him a few questions?" Ray ran his fingers through his thick, brown facial hair. "Well, I believe on the way in, there was an old building on the outskirts of town that we passed. It looked pretty run down." Mavrick's eyes lit up. "I think I know the place you are talking about." Ray chimed in. "Yeah I, think that that will be a good spot; if nothing else, we can at least get a little rest." Mavrick nodded, and then all three of the men made their way to the small, abandoned building.

    It took the men about ten minutes to reach their destination, as both the outlaw and Mavrick were walking, and Ray kept a slow trot just in case he was needed. Once the men got to the house, Ray mentioned that he didn't remember it looking as worn on their way into town. Looking the place over from where they stood, they noticed that the windows on the front of the house were both broken. One of them was located on the second story to the right of the entrance. The other one was directly to the left of the door on the first story, and it looked like it had been boarded up as a way to keep people out of the home. The siding looked like it was composed of rustic old wood, grey as a cloudy day. The stains that covered most of it indicated age and experienced multiple storms. The roof was in even worse shape than the siding, providing a similar worn look, showing the abuse that it endured with time, along with the top right part of it being caved in.

Ray allowed himself to slide off the horse, then led Old Red over to the log fence that was barely standing. As he began hitching Old Red to the wooden plank, he couldn't help but be concerned with how much it shook. Pulling the reins tight, Ray looked Old Red in the eyes as he patted his mane, saying "Don't go running off anywhere, you hear?" Turning his attention toward Mavrick, he said "I'm gonna make my way around the place and try to figure out a way in." Mavrick nodded. "Okay, if you need anything, let me know." Ray passed the fence then started toward the left side of the home.

He noted that there were only two windows on this side of the house. Both were on the first floor and had been boarded up, but they were still in good condition. Making his way to the rear of the building, he saw four windows, similar to those on the side. The only difference that really struck Ray as odd was that the window to the bottom left of the four was missing one of the wooden planks that the others had. Ray placed his face up to it in an attempt at getting a peek of their future shelter. He could only see the dust that covered the window's pane and what little distorted the light was able to get through. Suddenly, the trees behind Ray started shaking wildly. He couldn't help but throw himself around quickly, drawing one of his Birds of Prey revolvers as he yelled out, "Who goes there?" Ray started treading slowly toward the part of the backyard, which began to transition into the treeline that preceded the swamp.

  Everything became eerily still except his heart, which was beating so hard that Ray felt as if it were going to burst out of his chest. The rustling started again, with the same intensity as before, just as Ray made it to the tree line. He then started shouting in a deep, stern voice. "I ain't asking again, who is here?" Ray attempted to conceal any signs of fear from leaking through. The only response was the tree becoming still once again. Without taking risks of walking closer, Ray leaned in and attempted to get a better look at who may have been there. Without warning, a raccoon shot out of the trees, hissing at Ray, causing him to jump and shoot off his revolver. Missing the raccoon, it snarled at him and then quickly scurried off in the other direction.

Mavrick's voice faintly traveled in the distance from behind Ray. "You okay?" Ray nodded as if Mavrick would have been able to see him do so. Meanwhile, he took a deep breath and yelled, "Yeah, I'm good." This action caused Ray to start coughing violently, so much so that he couldn't help but fall to his knees as he attempted to catch his breath. Gasping violently, Ray became dizzy for a moment, shook his head, and rubbed the side of his temple, murmuring to himself that everything was going to be okay. As he looked back up toward the tree line, he noticed a boot that was just barely sticking out among one of the tree trunks. After regaining his composure, Ray pulled himself back to his feet and treaded slowly toward the boot. Starting at the front part of the tree trunk, where he could only see the bottom half of it, Ray slowly followed the bark as it guided him to unveil what the boot was on.

Once he was standing in front of the tree and cautiously followed the trunk, which slowly unveiled the top portions of the black as dirt boots, followed by the legs, torso, and eventually the head. The thing that laid before

Ray was a putrefying corpse. The clothing it wore looked relatively nice, except for being torn. Its face didn't leave any trace of what it looked like before the orifices became littered with maggots. What was left of the corpse's skin was a pale green color and a smell so putrid that it made a concoction of rotten eggs and rotten meat smell pleasant in comparison.

Ray couldn't help but jump back when seeing the entire corpse. Part of him wondered if it was due to a small amount of him hoping it wasn't what he thought it was or if it was due to the overwhelming smell. Ray then pinched his fingers together over his nose and regained his composure as he searched the body over from a distance. He turned himself around and headed back toward Mavrick, making his way alongside the right part of the home.

As he walked past the old, torn-down building again, he glanced over the windows as did with the other sides. This side mimicked the opposite side to a T, not only in the number of windows but also in their position and how they were boarded up. Ray then walked back over to Mavrick, who still had a tight grip on the outlaw's shoulder. "So, what's the verdict?" Mavrick asked. "Well, the house seems empty; the easiest way in would most likely be through one of the windows in the back as it is missing one of its boards." Mavrick nodded. "Okay, why don't you go that route then. You can let us in once you get inside of the building." Ray quickly turned around while saying "Okay. " He then walked quickly toward the window that he was referring to.

    As he made it to the destination, Ray couldn't help but check over his shoulder multiple times just in case anyone had their eye on him. Once in front of the window, Ray attempted to open it outside by sliding it up. It wouldn't budge. Ray quickly looked around one more time to ensure no one was close enough to cause trouble. Seeing no one, he removed one of his revolvers from its holster. He pistol-whipped the window, causing it to shatter into multiple pieces. This action then gave Ray access to the board, blocking his entrance. Latching on to it with his hands, Ray shook it to feel how loose it was. After a few strong pulls, he determined the board was securely fastened. Readjusting his grip, he then used the top panel to hoist himself in through the window.

Ray treaded lightly across the floor toward the door out just on the chance of them not being alone. The old wooden door was latched with a wooden plank secured by a metal bracket on the wall. Ray attempted to pull up the wooden plank, but unfortunately, it was secure in place due to rust and time. "Damn, I have to get more leverage if I am going to get this door open." He said while inhaling a deep breath in an attempt to regain his composure and then squatting to better position himself for extra leverage. Ray then proceeded to lift with all the might that he currently possessed, so much so that his face became scrunched and red. Within seconds Ray started to shake from exhaustion. Finally, the plank began to give a little, and suddenly it shot out of the bracket holding it in place, flew sideways, and it slammed down to the floor, letting out a loud thud. "There you go, Mavrick." Ray said as he pulled the door open. "Much obliged, friend," Mavrick said while pushing the outlaw forward into the house.

Once the other two men were in the building, Ray shut the door and latched it by setting the wood back in place. The inside of the building was covered in a mixture of dust and dirt. The hardwood floor had many holes, indicating that the building had been abandoned for a substantial amount of time. If anyone made the slightest weight shift, creaks echoed through the room only to be received by the men. Ray assumed that it must have been the living room based on what little old furniture inhabited the space they walked into. This furniture was made up of two whiteish French Gold Gilt chairs, one peach-colored Sheraton sofa, and an Oak colored table in the middle of the room.

Ray made his way over to one of the chairs and collapsed into it out of exhaustion. Meanwhile, Mavrick took the outlaw over to the other seat that was directly across from Ray, "Sit down!" he growled as the outlaw struggled. "No, why should I? You guys already took me prisoner. The least y'all can do is let me stand." Mavrick then positioned him directly in front of the chair, "Okay." He said as he raised his foot, driving his heel straight into the chest of the outlaw. This caused him to fall back into the chair, almost making it tip over. Mavrick walked directly behind him, "If you move, you're dead, you hear me?" The outlaw just sat there staring at his feet. "Well, I would nod yes, but I prefer to live." Mavrick chuckled a little, saying "Funny guy." He then took some of the rope hanging from his shoulder and wrapped it around the outlaw six or seven times until he pulled the rope tight and then tied the ends into a knot.

Once the outlaw was secured, Mavrick then searched him for any weapons that he could find. He started with patting the outlaw down along the sides of his dirty clothes. The only things this led to him finding were his revolver in the outlaw's holster hanging off the side of a belt and a small, jagged hunting knife. The blade was being held snug against his hip by the belt. Mavrick took both weapons along with the outlaw's bandanna and hat. He then placed them over on the table where Ray could keep an eye on them and then ambled over to the couch and sat down. "Well, man, there ain't no way you are going to get out of that," Mavrick said while smirking. The man looked like he was in his early twenties, had green eyes, a long nose with a narrow bridge, and his hair was dishwater blonde and parted on the top right side. His hair's length in the front came down to the tip of his nose, and the back's length came down to the height of his jawline.

Ray was glaring at the outlaw. "So tell me who you are." The outlaw's eyes mirror Ray's. "The name is Gabriel, Gabriel Celestino." Ray pulled his peacemaker out and aimed it at him. "Why are you robbing people, Gabriel?" The outlaw rolled his eyes as a smirk came across his face. "I guess you could say mommy issues." Ray sighed. "You think you're funny, huh?" he said, slightly moving his hand toward the right and pulling the trigger. The shot went off, and it whizzed right next to Gabriel's ear. "I recommend you start talking; I really hate to waste bullets." Gabriel's eyes opened up wide, and his face started to lose color. "Okay! Okay, I will tell you, damn! My family is originally from these parts. My Grandfather, Peter Celestino, moved to California during the gold rush. After striking gold, he came back with my father and lived out his days here."

Ray raised his voice." Boy, you really want to die, don't you? I asked why you are robbing banks, not for your life's story." Gabriel interrupted. "Wait, I'm getting to that part." Ray bit his lower lip out of frustration; it was clear that his patience was running thin. "As my father got older, he eventually met my mother, and naturally, that led me to be born. We were happy for the most part until my mother became deathly ill. Out of desperation, my father used most of our family's fortune in an attempt to save her." Mavrick nodded his head, and a frown formed on his face. "You know Ray, I think this son of a bitch is just trying to buy as much time as possible." Gabriel's face became red, and his eyebrows proceeded to scrunch up tightly. "I ain't, I swear, I am getting there!" Mavrick removed a knife he had sheathed, grabbed the bottom part of his shirt, and started wiping the blade tip to the top of the handle. A slight grin came across his face. Gabriel continued, "Within a few months, my mother ended up succumbing to her illness. This led my father to develop a disease that deteriorated his liver and our financial well-being. After my father passed, I swore that one way, I would rebuild my family's wealth back to the fortune that luck had bestowed upon us."

"Within the week, I was at a local saloon, following in my father's footsteps, drinking away the sorrow that I had. While sitting at the bar, a fella came up to me, asking what was wrong. My lips had to have been looser than usual because I had just started consoling this stranger like he was a long-lost friend. I don't know if the guy took pity on me or struck up the conversation with me with the intent of recruiting. After a few hours, he offered me an opportunity to make my money back. Regardless, somehow we made it to this point." Ray started running his right hand through his facial hair. "Okay, so what gang are you running with? Who is your leader?" Gabriel's eyes grew wider. "If I tell you, I'm signing my own death warrant." Mavrick threw himself off the couch, pulling his revolvers out of their holsters, and aimed them directly at Gabriel's face. "If you don't talk, you realize that you are also signing your death warrant." Gabriel became paler than a ghost, and his eyes shot back and forth like a mouse trapped between two cats. "Ok, I'll talk… The gang is called the Hangman's Gallows, and the leader's name is Peter Gun."

    Ray's and Mavrick's eyes met each other as the look of concern made itself apparent on their faces through the raised eyebrows and the dropped jaws. "Give us a moment Gabriel." Ray said as he stood up and waved to Mavrick to follow him to the other side of the house. Once both men entered the kitchen, Mavrick quickly blurted out, "What the hell man, you heard him say the Hangman's Gallows!" Ray leaned back against the sink. "Yeah, unfortunately, I did. Based on your response, I am going to assume you are familiar with them too?" Mavrick raised one eyebrow, "No shit, the Hangman's Gallows is one of the most notorious gangs across all of the United States. There ain't a state that they haven't been active in from my understanding." Ray pulled his hat off and ran his fingers through his hair, "Mavrick, what are we going to do? Word of the guy we killed will get back to their leader in the gang, and they ain't going to be happy. On top of that, if they find out that we are the ones that shot him, they are going to reign down hell on us." Mavrick sighed as Ray reached a handout and placed it on Mavrick's right shoulder. "Don't worry, it will all work out." Mavrick reciprocated, nodding his head slowly.

"So, what should we do about the boy?" Mavrick asked. "Well, for the time being, let's keep him tied up so he can't do us any harm. At least until we figure out a way to get rid of him without placing targets on our backs." Mavrick nodded as he headed out the kitchen doorway, back to the room where Gabriel had been left as Ray followed in his footsteps. "So what are you guys going to do, kill me?" Gabriel asked, a tremble in his voice as Mavrick smirked, "Maybe." Ray then walked over to the door looking out one of the barred-up windows, "You know, Mavrick, it may not be a bad idea to fix up this place a bit and stay here, even if only for a little while. Maybe I should head out and get some tools before it gets too late." Mavrick nodded. "Go for it boss. I will keep an eye on this dumb son of a bitch." Ray then pulled up the wood that barred the door and made his way toward Old Red. He then unhitched him, pulled himself up, and rode off to take care of the task at hand.

Chapter 11 Hammers, Nails, and Voodoo

Ray pulled back up to the general store, which he was at a couple of hours prior. He made his way off Old Red and hitched him up to one of the posts located just a couple steps away from the building's entrance. Walking into the building, a slight smile came across the shopkeeper's face as he teased Ray. "Forget something, friend?" Ray tipped his hat to him. "Actually, yes. Do y'all by chance have any hammers and nails?" The shopkeeper nodded and rummaged around under the front wooden counter that he was standing behind. After a few moments, he pulled out a small box of nails and a hammer. Ray let out a sigh of relief. "How much?" The shopkeeper's eyes wandered around as he thought about it for a moment. " The hammer is twenty-four cents, the box of nails is also twenty-four cents. So, this will run you forty-eight cents."

Ray started rummaging around through his satchel for a moment until he found a handful of coins. He then placed them on the store's counter and said "That should be enough to cover it." A woman around her mid-forties then walked into the store and browsed around. She stood out to him as she wore a large bandanna upon her head, which kept most of her coarse, black, curly hair covered. Another thing that caught Ray's attention was her massive rings and bracelets. He found it interesting that almost all of them had the same golden talisman etched into them that many of the surrounding gates in the area shared.

　　　After counting the change, the shopkeeper placed most of it in the register and handed two the coins back, as he gratefully said "Thanks again for your purchase, sir. Also, thank you again for taking care of those outlaws. You really helped me out back there." Before Ray had a chance to respond, the woman rushed up next to him at the counter and proceeded to cut him off. "Excuse me, I hate to be rude, but did you say this fella took care of some outlaws?" Her caramel-colored eyes had a slight glimmer in them from how the light hit them. "You wouldn't by chance know who these outlaws are, do you?" Ray's eyebrows scrunched up, bit his lower lip, and let out a deep breath. "You know, can't say that I do." His look went from concerned to confused as he brought his hand to his chin.

　　　"I'm sorry, who are you again?" She walked closer to Ray, so much so that their noses were mere inches away from each other. She then picked a piece of hair off of his jacket and proceeded to let go, allowing it to gently float to the floor as a slight frown came across her face. "My apologies, I didn't mean to be so forward. My name is Geneviéve Vigoureux. I live on the northern end of the city on the outskirts, in the swamps. My home has a set of wind chimes set equally apart from the stairs, and you can see a symbol painted on the door in red paint. The symbol looks like a diamond that extends out into two half diamonds and contains six dots surrounding it. If you learn anything of these outlaws, please stop by and let me know." The woman slowly strolled out the door and headed off toward the right. "That was weird," Ray thought to himself as he proceeded to thank the shopkeeper as he intended to do moments early and made his way back out to Old Red. After reaching his steed, he placed both the hammer and the box of nails into his pouch, unhitched the horse, and pulled himself up on top. He then pulled the reins, positioning Old Red in the direction of the old house.

Promptly, Ray found himself outside the old house, hitching his horse to one of the fence posts outside and then making his way inside. After walking through the door, Ray made his way over to the room that had the furniture. He then took the nails and hammer out of his satchel, placing them on the table. Mavrick kept his eyes locked in on Gabriel while asking Ray "How did everything go?" Ray found the empty chair and allowed his body to go limp, collapsing back into it. Before getting even a syllable out, he was attacked with a small coughing fit. Once he regained his composure, Ray answered Mavrick. "Well, getting everything wasn't a problem. However, I bumped into this weird middle-aged woman who gave me the creeps." Ray took his hat off for a moment and ran his hand through his thick, long, brown hair. "I think she said her name was Geneviéve Vigoureux or something like that."

Gabriel's eyes became as wide as a wagon's wheel, his face became gaunt, and his skin became increasingly pale. "What is it?" Mavrick interrogated Gabriel, taking instant notice of the grim change in demeanor. "That woman is bad news. I mean terrible news. We need to stay far away from her." His voice began trembling at the thought of the woman, but not quite nearly as violently as his body did. Ray intervened. "What do you mean?" Gabriel started laughing nervously while the other two men looked at him like he was going nuts. "Th… th...that woman is the Voodoo queen of Saint Edgerton." Ray placed his hat back on his head. "So, what does that have to do with us?"

Gabriel's laughing stopped dead in its tracks. "Probably nothing unless she finds out that you have me captive." Ray's eye's started squinting as if closely analyzing his face for any signs of lies. "You sure, you ain't just saying hogwash to get out of the bind you are in?" Gabriel's face lost all expression. His eyes teared up as he stared back into Ray's. "I wish I was. The outlaws that I ran with robbed a local saloon her husband ran. While we were there, he acted like he was going to surrender only to pull a shotgun out from under the bar. Unfortunately, he tried to be a hero and took a shot at one of our gang's leaders. Without thinking, I pulled my revolver out." Gabriel looked down; his facial expressions and tone of voice painted a picture of how remorseful he truly was. "I shot him dead."

Ray turned away for a moment, scrunching up his eyes in disgust. "I see, so why don't we just hand you over to her?" Mavrick grew that wild smirk that he was starting to become notorious for as he turned his head toward Ray, his eyes remaining locked on Gabriel, clearly watching for his reaction. "You know Ray, that is a great idea." Gabriel's face lost all color once again. "No, please! Like I told you guys before, that woman is bad news! Trouble follows her wherever she goes!" Mavrick chuckled. "I would say so because we are going to hand you over to her." Gabriel interrupted once again. "There has to be something I can do to convince you otherwise." Ray turned back around, facing Gabriel once again. "Well, possibly, do you by chance know Travis Fowler?" Gabriel shook his head, "I don't think so. Why?" Ray let out a sigh. "Well, he is the reason we are here in the first place. We have been tracking down that son of a bitch." Gabriel's face lit up, a small glimmer of hope shining through. "I may be able to help you track them down. The gang I run with has branches that lead all over the country, but the base of it is right here in Saint Edgerton." Ray started running his fingers through his beard, "I don't know."

Suddenly, a loud thud that sounded like a sack of potatoes could be heard hitting the window. This noise seemed to have originated from the window to the right of the door's position from inside. "What the hell was that?" Mavrick asked, pulling his guns from their holsters as Ray made his way back to his feet. "Stay here. I'm going to check it out." He instructed Mavrick as he drew the birds of prey revolvers and placed his body against the wall for cover. He then utilized the butt of the revolver in his left hand to open the door slightly. "Shit, I can't see anything." Ray muttered to himself under his breath. He then released a breath so deep, Mavrick and Gabriel could feel the anxiety and uncertainty radiating off of it. Mavrick, with concern in his voice, asked, "Ray, would you like me to go out there instead?" Ray's eyebrows scrunched together, and a frown found its way on his face, displaying a slight annoyance. "Don't worry, I got it." he snapped back as he pulled himself away from the wall, kicking open the door.

Ray made his way out onto the porch with his revolvers at the ready. He then turned to the left, looking at the window where the sound came from, searching for any indication of the source. From a glance, there was nothing that Ray could spot. He then analyzed the porch to see if he could pinpoint what caused the sound. On the old, torn-up wooden floor, a few inches from the middle of the window, laid the corpse of a crow. Its wings were spread wide, and its head dangled unnaturally from its body. "Poor son of a bitch." Ray muttered to himself as he looked up toward the lawn, noticing millions of bird bodies lying on the lawn surrounding the house. "Something ain't right," Ray told himself as he treaded slowly down the porch. Looking past the fence, he couldn't help but be astonished at the fact that not one bird was lying on the ground past the barrier. Ray took another glance at the crow that laid limp on the porch and pondered to himself how weird it was that it was the only one of all of the birds that seemed to succumb to a violent end. He then cautiously made his way through the field of birds, attempting to avoid stepping on any of the corpses while making his way to the backyard. Once the full yard was in view, Ray let out a shocked gasp as he was blown away with the foul sight of every inch of the yard up to the tree line being covered to the brim with crows.

    The tree line that shook earlier from the raccoon caught Ray's attention again as it began shaking, only this time far more violently. Usually, something like this wouldn't bother him too much. Still, with the birds surrounding him like a mob and what Gabriel told them, his anxiety was in full gear. Ray took a deep breath, attempting to calm his nerves. "Okay, this is most likely a raccoon just like last time." he reassured himself, whispering under his breath. The tree's branches continued to shake as if it was attempting to withstand a mighty windstorm. Exasperation overtook him at this point, causing him to loosen his lips and shout, "Get out of here, you damn varmint!" The outline of a man emerged from the shaking trees. Ray's expectation of a small critter shooting out from the wooded area was completely thrown off, leading him to aim down the sights of the birds of prey. "What the hell are you doing out here, mister?" he yelled in a deep growl.

The only response Ray was met with was a few faint grunts as slowly it limped toward him. More detail of the figure's hideous decay came to light the closer it got. Its skin was a pale green, almost grey color. Where its eyes should have been were dark sockets that seemed to be completely hollowed out. This was except for the white wiggling pile of maggots that resided at the bottom of each eye hole. Ray noticed that the clothes he found on this one seemed identical to those on the corpse he saw earlier. "You gotta be shitting me." Ray barely managed to whisper to himself over the frog in his throat, as his body trembled and he paled, causing him to look like a ghost. "Freeze, or I will shoot!" His command thundered through the air as he started to shake off his state of shock.

The zombie's hands continued to reach out as it continued; it slowly staggered toward him. Ray could hear a slight moan escaping its oral cavity. "Final chance!" Ray yelled. The creature just continued forward, ignoring his demands. He then shot off both of the revolvers; the bullet from the right one hit the being in the left shoulder, while the bullet from the left chamber hit it in the chest. This caused it to stagger back for a moment but then continued forward as if it was only a flesh wound. Ray's jaw lowered in disbelief as his eyes became wider. He pulled the hammers back with his thumbs and pulled the trigger again, letting off two more shots. This time, the bullet from the left one ended up hitting the zombie's hand while the right one shot directly in the middle of its throat. Much like before, this caused the zombie to stagger back a bit. This seemed to be a mere inconvenience creature as it was back on the path as if nothing had happened within seconds.

      Overwhelmed with shock and disbelief, Ray could not look away from the zombie, which was now a few steps away from him. He proceeded to walk backward to distance himself from the grotesque creature. However, as Ray took his third step, he placed his foot on one of the crow corpses that covered the ground. This caused him to lose his balance and almost fall; however, he could redeem himself. After regaining his balance, Ray reholstered his guns and then unsheathed his knife. Ray then lunged toward the monster, thrusting his blade as hard as he could up through the bottom of the jaw of the creature. The empty shell of a man's mouth became locked in place with the knife.

Ray realized that the knife was lodged in place, so he placed his left hand over his right and forced the blade's handle upward, causing the creature to look up into the sky. While doing this, the creature's hands attempted to grab onto Ray's shoulders, but before it could get a grip, Ray was quick enough to sidestep to the zombie's right side. He then kicked it in the back of its right knee, causing it to stumble to the ground. While it was going down, Ray pulled the blade out of its jaw, flipped it around, placing it in the icicle position. The zombie's body hit the ground, sounding like a wet bag of potatoes hitting the ground. He then thrust it down toward the creature's head with all of his might, yelling, "Die, you dead son of a bitch!" as the blade fought its way through the decaying flesh and bone. In conjunction with the sound, the smell pushed Ray to the point of disgust, causing him to gag.

Once he regained his composure, the tree line caught his glance yet again. What was different from last time was that multiple small trees and bushes seemed to be shaking violently versus the one. Ray's face was gaunt, pale, and wide-eyed due to the sight of the figures swarming out of the swamps. The group of them seemed to be endless; as one stumbled toward him, another creature would emerge from the tree line to take its place. Ray began to notice that, like the zombie he had just dealt with, all of the figures he could see seemed to be missing chunks of flesh. This caused Ray to stumble back a few steps; the look on his face became permeated with the look of fear. So many zombies were flooding out of the swamps he began to lose count. This is when he turned around and ran back into the house to let the other two know what was happening.

    The old wooden door burst open with such force that when it slammed against the wall, the sound of a loud crack filled the room. This caught both men in the room off guard and caused Mavrick to draw his revolvers toward the door before he realized that Ray was the cause of the sudden noise. "What the hell was that for Ray! You realize I could have shot you dead, right?" Ray quickly turned around, placed the wooden plank back in place to lock the door, and turned toward Mavrick. Ray's face maintained that distraught look that he had outside the house, and he pointed his right hand's index finger toward the kitchen's back wall. "Mavrick, we have a real problem! There are a ton of zombies coming out of the swamps behind the house, and call it a hunch, but I have a feeling that they are headed here. We need to either run or fight." Mavrick ran over to a window, squinted his eyes as he pressed his face against it. "Oh shit, you ain't kidding around. Well, boss, I'll stand my ground if you will." Ray nodded, "Okay, just a heads up, the only way I was able to kill one of these things was to stab it in the head." Mavrick exhaled deeply. "Gotcha." he said, unsheathing his knife in his right hand and unholstering his revolver in his left.

Ray followed suit, withdrawing his right revolver along with his knife. "This is somehow tied to that witch! Gabriel chimed in. "Untie me guys, I will be able to help!" Mavrick looked at Ray, his facial expression asking for reassurance. "That that would be the best move, and y'all know it!" Gabriel continued. Ray glared at him with a slight smirk on his face. "Now why would we do that when you seem so comfy sitting there." Realizing that he was trapped like a mouse in a viper pit, Gabriel started shaking violently like a leaf on a tree does during a storm. *Thud! Thud! Thud! The* sound of the creature's limbs making contact with the wooden siding of the old house and the sound echoed through the inside. Ray looked at Mavrick. "You ready?" He just nodded. With each thud, the board that held the door in place started to gain an additional crack until it finally succumbed to the overwhelming pressure of the creatures against the entrance.

Crack! The door flew open, causing its back to slam against the inner wall. The creatures started to flood the room so rapidly that when one moved forward, another one took its place immediately. Ray and Mavrick started open-firing, but all it seemed to do was slow down the relentless creatures. The first one that shambled in finally reached the grappling distance of Ray. Before it could latch on, Ray stepped back a few steps and shot the creature point-blank in between the eyes. This caused its head to jerk back violently while its body followed as it fell to the ground. At this point, Mavrick had two of those monsters coming at him. One was roughly ten feet away, while the closer one was around five feet away. He took four shots, each bullet taking out a kneecap of the Zombies, causing both of their cold decaying bodies to collapse forward, racing to the floor. Once on the ground, he shot both of them in the head, using the last two bullets in the chamber of his right Revolver, "Son of a bitch, I need to reload!" Mavrick growled.

Ray had three creatures surrounding him at this point; they were all reaching out toward him as they slowly closed in around him. His eyes shuffled wildly between them. Ray reassured Mavrick. "Go for it. I'll cover you." Ray kicked the zombie to his left, causing it to collapse forward under its own body weight. The instant the creature was about waist high to Ray, he thrust his knife through its jaw, locking it closed. He then aimed the revolver in his left hand directly at the zombie that shambled toward him on his right. Ray thrust down violently with his right hand, which removed his knife and utilized the momentum from the bodyweight of the creature. This caused it to hit the ground violently. At the same time, Ray pulled the trigger, lodging a bullet directly between the eyes of the zombie on his right. Its head jerked back violently. Ray then adjusted his aim slightly to the left while pulling the hammer back on the revolver and fired off a shot at the creature down his sight. While the bullet penetrated the eye socket of that zombie, the one that Ray stabbed earlier proceeded to get back up. Ray saw this happening, flipped the knife around to the icicle position, and thrust it down into the back of the skull of this creature. The corpse fell to the ground letting out a *Thud*!

Gabriel was hyperventilating, tears filling up his eyes like a well overflowing. "Please, you have to let me out of here! I have no way of defending myself!" Ray shouted back, with a mocking tone underlying his words, as the hoard of the undead continued to flood the room. "Don't you worry, sweetheart. We ain't gonna let anything happen to you, isn't that right, Mavrick?" Mavrick couldn't help but smirk, even with five of the creatures surrounding him at that point. "You know it Ray." he said as he threw his knife back in the sheath and drew his other revolver. He pulled back both hammers and went right down the line, starting with the zombies at the end of each side. Mavrick alternated shots, aiming with care to hit them in the head until he reached the last one in the middle. For that zombie, he took his left revolver and placed it in the hollowed-out cavity of the jawbone. Looking at the creature in the frosted-over eye, Mavrick pulled the trigger. What remained of the creature's head flew back violently, falling to the ground. Once it hit the wooden planks of the floor, it let out a loud thud.

This left a small gap between the zombies and Ray, allowing him to push forward a bit. He could only make it a few steps closer to the door before six of those creatures completely surrounded him. Ray thrust his knife into the creature's temple to the far left while simultaneously shooting the one farthest to the right. He then kicked forward the one in the middle, causing it to stumble back a few steps. Due to the momentum from falling into the kick, Ray started stumbling forward. He fell toward the undead creature to the diagonal right of him as he was trying to catch his balance. Due to how quickly he ran into it, it fell backward while Ray fell to the floor. The zombie that was to the left of him at this point threw its bony claw back and unhinged its mandible, letting out a soft hissing sound. Ray's eyes widened as he yelled out in fear. "Mavrick, Help!" The creature swung its claw toward Ray at such a fast speed, he swore this was going to be it for him. The claw made it so close to his eye that if it had been any closer, It would have punctured it. Before it had a chance to do so, however, the zombie's arm jerked violently toward the left, following its body and head, or what was left of it after the revolver round pierced the skull.

    Ray utilized his momentum to flip him over to his stomach; he then pushed the sides of his full fists into the ground and pressed against it, allowing him to force his body up. As he got to his knees, two of the undead creatures loomed over Ray. The one that was to the right let its mandible hang open as it leaned in to take a chunk out of him, only to get a mouth full of his heated-up revolver muzzle. Ray then pulled the trigger, and the skull exploded like TNT going off, shattering chips of bone and flesh every which way. The other creature latched onto Ray's arm that was still extended out, digging its rotten teeth so deep into his forearm that it almost made contact with the bone. Ray couldn't help but yell out in pain as the revolver fell from his hand and hit the wooden floor, which almost sounded like a heavy hammer falling at full force on a solid piece of oak. He then took the knife that was in his other hand and plunged it down in the decomposing cranium of the undead creature, causing it to release the grip that it had on him.

It fell to the ground while Ray scurried back to Mavrick's location, keeping a tight grip on the wound to help stop the bleeding. The creatures continued to pour into the building while Mavrick continued to take them out one shot after another. Ray sat down, grabbed hold of his shirt's sleeve with his teeth, and used his knife to cut it down to where the zombie bit into his flesh. Once he made it to that area, Ray used the knife to cut at the sleeve of his shirt until the fabric could be pulled apart. With the sleeve hanging from his teeth, Ray looked at his wound closer and released his grip allowing the piece of tattered clothing to fall on his lap as he started gagging. A small group of maggots crawled and wiggled around in the wound. Ray couldn't help but shake violently due to the combination of pain and disgust that filled his body.

After a few seconds, he started to overcome the initial shock. Placing the knife down with his good hand as he flung open the top latch of his brown leather satchel and rummaged around in it for a moment. Quickly he removed a small silver flask concealed amongst some of the other things in his sack and placed it directly in between his legs. Ray then used them to grip the flask, holding it in place as he utilized his hand on his uninjured arm to twist the top off. Meanwhile, the sound of Mavrick's bullets continued to whiz through the air, releasing a wet cracking noise as it pierced the flesh and bones of the decaying corpses that continued to shuffle toward them. With the top of the flask dangling from the small metal piece that kept it from getting lost, Ray flipped the flask over as he yelled out in agony. Offering his wound, a little bit of his moonshine worked as Ray had hoped. It instantly killed the maggots and caused their remains to float out of the injury.

Ray then took the part of his sleeve lying in his lap and placed the middle of the cloth directly over the wound. When it rested it the faint outline of the injury pressed itself against the piece of clothing. Gabriel was doused in sweat at this point and couldn't help but hyperventilate. "Guys, please let me out to help. I can help! I swear, I won't try to run!" Ray and Mavrick's eyes met each other as they nodded simultaneously in agreement. Ray placed the cap back on the flask, tightened it to the best of his ability, and slid it back into his satchel. He then extended his hand out, meeting Mavricks, who helped pull him up. Once he was on his feet, Ray made his way to where Gabriel sat and looked him straight, dead in the eye. "Listen, we are going to let you loose, to give us a hand. If you try to run or do anything funny, Mavrick or I will shoot you down so fast that it will make lightning look slower than a seven-year itch." Ray's face displayed sincerity along with exhaustion as it was covered with sweat and his eyes were cold. "Understand?"

Gabriel nodded in agreement. Mavrick glanced over for a moment between taking shots and sarcastically jabbed at the two of them. "You ladies done kissing yet? I only ask because I really need help" Ray took his knife out and instructed Gabriel to lean forward slightly. Once done, he placed the blade on the inside of the rope, in between Gabriel's tied hands, and set the serrated blade snug against the rope. After a few strong swipes with the knife, the frayed pieces of the rope fell to the ground. "Thanks." Gabriel said. His face lit up, overjoyed that he was no longer bound up like some sort of prisoner. Ray looked him dead in the eye once again. "Don't thank me just yet. We got to still get out of here alive. Your weapons are on the table. Grab them and help us out." Ray then turned around, only to see the doorway flooding with what now seemed like an endless horde of the undead. Mavrick yelled out, his voice trembling with the certainty that the odds were stacked against them. "Guys, I really need help here!" Ray pulled out his Birds of Prey revolvers once again, joining Mavrick in his pursuits to turn the tide of the unfavorable odds. Mavrick stood his ground to the left while Ray took to the right, and Gabriel joined in open firing on whatever seemed to get past the other two men. With gunsmoke filling the air, it became harder to make out the exact details of the creatures at this point.

Gabriel made it through his fully loaded revolver rounds only to realize that he had no more ammo on him. "Son of a bitch, I'm fresh out of rounds! Do you guys have any extra bullets I could use?" Ray shook his head while Mavrick scoffed and told him just to stay out of the way. Gabriel, now annoyed with the lack of assistance, started looking around the home to find a way to continue in the fight. Due to the loud noise made by the bullets going off mixed with the undead horde, Gabriel could make his way back to the old kitchen without Ray or Mavrick knowing. Once there, he began frantically searching the drawers to find anything that could be of assistance. Flinging open the fourth drawer down from the countertop, he discovered an old knife lying in there, which due to the blanket of dust that covered it showing, that it had been there for a while. "This is better than nothing." he said while slipping his revolver back in his holster and picking up the knife.

PSHHHHH! The glass shattered inward for the back windows in the kitchen. Gabriel grabbed a sharp piece of glass that lay broken on the floor. Without any warning, the wooden planks that composed the frame of the windows began to splinter and crack from the excess pressure. "Ohhh shit!" Gabriel said as he snatched up a sharp piece of broken glass that lay on the floor and sprinted back to where Ray and Mavrick were holding back the undead. "Guys, we are in some serious trouble! Those freaks are coming in through the windows in the back." The men could hear the hollow sound of wood making an impact, with the kitchen floor letting out a thud with each piece that hit it. Ray glanced toward the kitchen and then at Mavrick. At this point, he was scowling at him, "How the hell are we going to kill all of these monsters? They seem to be endless." Mavrick shook his head, "Honestly, I don't think we can; we are going to need to look for an opening and try to run."

    The creatures continued pouring into the old building while the sound of their decaying flesh making contact with the wooden floor filled the kitchen at an ever-increasing rate. Gabriel noticed that a few of the creatures were starting to fill the hallway at this point. Fear overtook him at this point as he walked over to the corner living room, where the hall and the wall meet. His eyes were wide, and his shirt was drenched in sweat due to the fear and anticipation that filled him. Getting his nerves under control, Mavrick forced himself in the middle of the hallway entrance, only to be merely two or three feet away from a creature that was shambling toward him. Gabriel then readied the knife in his right hand and the piece of glass in his left hand, both of which he held in an icicle position. Before the zombie closest to him could take a step into the living room, Gabriel lunged forward, swinging the knife to take a cut out of the creature's jugular area. Without any hesitation, he took his left hand and thrust it down upon the top of the creature's skull, causing it to collapse to the ground. The creature released a slight shallow moan as it fell to the ground producing a thud.

    The stairs right of Gabriel caught his attention for a moment before the line of zombies ahead of him gained it again. Crossing his arms, Gabriel allowed the zombie nearest to him to shamble into swinging distance of his weapons, impaling it on the left side of the creature's temple. He then used his knife's serrated blade to slit the creature's throat and proceeded to stab the zombie three times in the other side of its head. As the creature collapsed to its knees, Gabriel yelled back to Ray and Mavrick. "Guys, there are too many of these things. Even with them being slow, it's like when one dies another, two takes its place." Gabriel removed the piece of glass from the undead creature's skull, turned his body slightly, and side kicked the zombie backward. This dislodged his blade from the creature as its body made contact with the floor. "Maybe we should try to make it out from the top floor."

Ray responded while reloading his Birds of Prey revolvers. "That may not be a bad idea. I only have about twelve more rounds for the revolvers and an unpolished box of ammo for my shotgun." Realizing how much more grave the situation was becoming by the second, Mavrick nodded in agreement while continuing fire. "Yeah, I know what you mean. I'm starting to run low as well." Ray placed the final bullet in the chamber of his right revolver, slid the cylinder back in place, and spun it. "Okay, Gabriel, it looks like we are going to go with your plan. Continue to hold off those creatures from the hallway if you can. I will make my way over now. Mavrick, once I'm there, I will give you cover fire. Use it to sprint up the stairs, and we should be able to make it in one piece." Mavrick nodded his head, saying "Okay."

Ray then exhaled as he lurched toward the stairs, stopping only once reaching the wall next to the entryway. He then planted his back against it, bringing his revolvers to the ready, and yelled, "Mavrick, make your way over! I got you covered!" Mavrick sprinted to where the two men were stationed and headed up the steps. "Gabriel, let's go!" Ray commanded, following up the stairs behind Mavrick. Gabriel jerked his knife out of the last zombie that challenged him and kicked one at the front of the hoard backward, effectively causing some of the others to trip over it. Buying him a little more time, Gabriel turned around and sprinted up the stairs, following the steps of the other two men.

Chapter 12 Escaping the House of Dread

    Every step up the stairs released a loud creaking sound from the floorboards as if trying to notify the hoard of their location. Once finally at the top, the men found themselves in the entryway of the upstairs hall. Ray turned around to the old wooden door, which seemed to be the only thing that separated the stairs from the hall and forced it closed. He then leaned into the door with as much force as possible while instructing Mavrick and Gabriel to go into one of the rooms and see if they could find anything to place in front of the door. Both men scurried to the door at the end of the hall on the right and found an old bedroom. " Hurry guys, it sounds like these things are already halfway up the stairs!" Ray's voice echoed through the hall and made its way into the room where the men were looking around.

    While there wasn't a lot in the room, it did have a worn, full-size bed with three small holes scattered across the top of the mattress. Slightly to the left of it stood an old wooden wardrobe that matched the color and texture of the bed frame. "Perfect!" Mavrick stated ecstatically, "Gabriel, help me move this wardrobe out the doorway." Mavrick slid his revolvers back in their holsters as Gabriel nodded, acknowledging his request. Gabriel then made his way to the other side of the wardrobe, preparing himself. "Get ready, I'm going to bring the top down to you," Mavrick said as Gabriel slid the knife and broken piece of glass into his pockets and placed his hands against the top part of the dark brown wardrobe.

Ray started shouting, his voice filled to the brim with fear as it trembled, "Guys, these undead bastards are beating on the door, I can't hold it much longer! Hurry up!". Mavrick peeked around the corner of the wardrobe to catch a glimpse of Gabriel's face mirroring his as he asked, "On the count of three?" Only the right part of Gabriel's face could be seen nodding as he responded, "One, two, three!". The top of the wardrobe slowly lowered until it rested securely in Gabriel's hands. At the same time, Mavrick picked it up from the bottom, raising it to a comfortable height to maintain his grip. Both men started to move to their final destination, struggling with every step to produce more than a few grunts. Once they made it back to where Ray was positioned. Mavrick crouched down, slowly lowering his end of the wardrobe to the floor. With one edge of the bottom of the wardrobe securely on the floor, Gabriel brought his side of it up until it was standing upright.

"Okay, Gabriel," Mavrick said, "Come to the front of the wardrobe with me, and when Ray moves out of the way, we are going to push this thing with all we got." Gabriel nodded as both men positioned themselves against the wardrobe, placing their hands about shoulder-width apart and leaning into it. Mavrick then called out to Ray, "You ready bu-" before he could get a word out, Ray became overwhelmed with another coughing fit. This caused him to interrupt Mavrick and loosen his leverage on the door, which allowed the undead creatures to force it open. Thankfully, Ray was able to regain enough of his composure enough to be able to reposition his weight. This only allowed one of the zombies to be able to slip its decaying hand through the door's opening.

Mavrick yelled at Ray, "Move!" Ray pushed himself off the door without hesitation, causing him to stumble back quickly. Partially due to the momentum and the fatigue from attempting to catch his breath in between coughs, he lost his balance and started falling back. Ray was flailing his arms around wildly like a madman until he was finally able to regain his composure. Leaning forward, Ray placed his hands on his knees to brace himself for a moment. "I'm" *cough cough* "good" before he was able to get another cough out, the sound of the door creaking open began to flood the room. This slowly loosened the door's grip on the creature's arm, allowing for more of the arm to be exposed. Mavrick yelled, "Push!" Both Gabriel and he pushed with all their might, slamming the wardrobe into the door. Not only did this produce the loud sound of hollow wood hitting wood, but also a loud crack. This was followed by a thud as the arm lodged between the door and the frame became severed. It then fell to the floor and began twitching erratically.

    Both men slowly let the pressure off of the wardrobe, wanting to ensure that there would be enough resistance to prevent the undead horde from being able to force their way through. Once they ultimately had their hands off the wardrobe, it was clear that it wasn't going anywhere, so Gabriel walked over to the nearest wall and leaned against it. Mavrick used this opportunity to check on Ray. He was sitting with his back against the wall in a feeble attempt to gain control of his persistent cough. "You okay?" Mavrick asked Ray, who simply nodded no. Ray attempted to speak during the lows of the coughing fit "It is" cough *cough* "getting harder" *cough cough cough* "for me to breath and" *cough cough* "these damn coughing fits seem to be getting worse" *cough cough*. Ray pulled his hand away from his mouth after that last cough to see a small splatter of blood on the side of his hand.

After taking a few deep breaths, Ray was finally able to get it under control. He then removed a handkerchief from his satchel and wiped his hand off, removing the blood that covered it. Mavrick then reached his hand out, offering it to Ray as assistance to hoist him off the ground. After a slight moment of hesitation, he accepted it, securing a grip around Mavrick's forearm with his hand on his good arm. After being pulled by him, Ray took a second to regain his composure, letting out a deep sigh. "You guys get that the wardrobe ain't going to hold those bastards back for long, right?" Mavrick and Gabriel acknowledged his question with a nod which was followed by Mavrick asking Gabriel, "Would you mind looking out the window, from the room that we got the wardrobe from, and see what we have to get past to get out of this shithole?" Mavrick then turned his attention back to Ray. "While he looks that way, I will check out the room on the other side to see if there is a way out; you just rest up.

Ray moved over toward the wardrobe, sitting down on the floor in front of it as the other two men made their way to the area where they had planned on searching. Getting a glance out of the window, Gabriel's face couldn't help but become pale as his jaw dropped. What he saw was a hoard of undead creatures swarming the house. They were packed shoulder to shoulder, like a bunch of sardines packed in a can. To make matters worse, the horde seemed to stretch all the way out to the street. Gabriel checked the top of the window to ensure it was unlocked, and after a few strong jerks, he was finally able to force it open. Allowing Gabriel to get a better look at the outside of the house, he realized an excellent opportunity to use the top of the porch, which was located directly under the window. This would be a perfect spot to break their fall to the ground. "Now, if only I can figure out a way to get past these things. "Holy shit!" Mavrick's voice echoed through the mostly empty halls. Ray yelled back, "Everything okay?" Mavrick hollered in response, "I definitely wouldn't say that. We have an army of those undead bastards ranging from the swamps. Every time one moves forward, it's as if another one takes its place!"

Mavrick looked through the window thoroughly to look for any potential escape route that may have been missed. However, all this did was increase the reality of their situation to him. Mavrick let out a loud sigh, driven by the feeling of hopelessness. He proceeded to search the room to see if he could find anything of use. The room that Mavrick was in didn't offer much for him to look through, except for an old wooden chest against the far wall that sat perpendicular to the window. Along with this was a dark brown old wooden cabinet with a padlock to its right. Mavrick started with the old chest. The only thing that kept him from getting inside it was an unlocked iron latched, resembling almost a coal-like color. Unlatching it and pulling open the lid, he was greeted by a pile of worn clothing, an old empty leather satchel that was stained due to constant use, and metal tins of kerosene oil. Mavrick shook both tins, and the sound of the liquid sloshing along with the feeling told him that both of them were almost, if not completely full.

He then grabbed the old satchel, placing both tins into it and hanging it off his left side. Mavrick's attention then diverted to the padlock that secured the cabinet's doors. First, he pulled it down to see if he could pull it loose. With this not working, he removed one of his revolvers from their holsters and muttered to himself as he fired off a shot, "Whatever is in this stupid thing is it, better be worth it." Hitting the lock just above the bottom of its shackle, he caused it to break apart and let out a loud thud as it made contact with the wooden floor. Mavrick then slid the revolver back into the holster and unsheathed his knife, wedging the blade in between the small gap between the left cabinet door and the one on the right. He then placed his hand's palm on the base of the blade and pressed the handle toward the cabinet's right door. This, in turn, caused him to pry open the door on the left. Finally open, Mavrick couldn't help but smirk a little as what he saw gave him some hope.

The cabinet was filled with twelve brown bottles, which looked as if they were full of some sort of liquid. Mavrick reached in, pulled one out, twisted the top, and took in a whiff of the unmarked liquid. His eyes widened, and his smirk grew even wider as he lifted the bottle to his lips, allowing a small amount of liquid to seep into his mouth. Mavrick's taste buds confirmed what he thought it was. He then pried open the other door to find some neatly folded blankets topped with a pile of dust. "Boys, I think I just came up with an idea!" His voice echoed through the mostly empty hall, shrouded in confidence. Overcome with curiosity, Ray's voice shaking from a combination of exhaustion and fear meant Mavrick, "What is it?". "Give me a moment, and I will show you."

He then proceeded to pull the blanket out of the wardrobe, which caused a cluster of .45 revolver rounds to fall to the ground. "What the hell?" Mavrick said, throwing the blanket off to the side. As he pulled out more of them, his face couldn't help but light up more as he was greeted by a stash of revolver round boxes stacked neatly and hidden away in the back. "Jackpot!" His voice was filled to the brim with excitement as it echoed through the halls. Ray could be heard letting out a quiet sigh as Gabriel asked the same thing he had asked earlier, "What is it?". Mavrick started filling his satchel with the boxes of bullets while responding. "Why don't you come see? After all, I could use some help carrying all of this." As Gabriel made his way toward the room, the hallway became extremely quiet except for the slight grunts and knocks coming from behind the door that led down the stairs. The swift sound of Gabriel's boots continued, increasing in sound until he was standing in the doorway. "Good, you're here. Take this over to the window in the room where you were just in." Mavrick handed

Gabriel the crate full of the bottles, and the liquid inside them could be heard swishing around. Gabriel then went back into the room, placing the containers next to the window.

Simultaneously, Mavrick grabbed as many of the blankets as he could, then hugged a massive pile of them securely to his chest. Knowing his grip on the blankets was stable enough so that they wouldn't fall, Mavrick slowly raised himself to a standing position and then walked carefully toward the window where Gabriel was waiting. He directed Ray to come along, making his way past the door where the wardrobe was placed against. Taking a deep breath and slowly exhaling, Ray weakly forced himself back up to his feet and then proceeded to follow Mavrick to the room. With all three men in the room, Mavrick shuffled through his satchel, pulling out six boxes of ammo. He then instructed both Ray and Gabriel to each take three boxes. The two men filled their satchels with the allotted ammo, and as Gabriel asked Mavrick, "What is the plan?"

Mavrick was quiet as he walked past them, making his way to the window. He then placed his hands under the lip allowing him to open it. Mavrick then turned to his right, bending over to grab a bottle from one of the Crates. Pulling it out with his right hand, he stood back up to a straight position looking at Gabriel with a slight smirk coming across his face, saying, "This is it.". Gabriel's eyes became wide, his face indicating he was trying to fully comprehend what was going through Mavrick's mind. Mavrick then drew his revolver in his left hand and tossed the bottle out of the window with his right one like a tomahawk. Mavrick took a shot with his gun as it flew through the air. This led to the sound of glass shattering and a blanket of fire consuming the alcohol, in turn falling on the hoard.

Gabriel's face lit up as he complimented him, saying, " Good thinking!" Mavrick acknowledged this with a simple nod of his hat. "Gabriel, Ray, I'm going to go out of the window; I should be able to stand on the roof of the porch. This should allow the two of you to have plenty of room to help me take care of these zombies. Ray, when I get out there, I need you to toss me a few bottles." He nodded, acknowledging what was asked of him. Once Mavrick was on the roof, Ray grabbed two bottles and handed them out the window to him. With a solid grip on them, he made his way to the far right of the porch, setting down the bottles, and started filling the chambers of the revolvers with the ammo from the boxes he just raided from the cabinet. Ray then informed Gabriel that he would do the same thing, and he cautiously followed Mavrick out the window.

Once Ray's feet were planted on the roof, Gabriel bent over, grabbing four of the bottles sitting in the bin. He placed two of the necks between his ring fingers and pinky fingers while the other two necks were resting between his thumbs and his index fingers. Gabriel then handed two of them to Ray, saying, "I will come out there with y'all, so Ray, if you would hold these two for me, I would appreciate it." Ray nodded, placing the two bottles at his feet, and reached out for the other two. As they meant Ray's empty hands, he bent over and gently placed them down on the top of the roof.

With the bottles in place, Ray stood back up, extending his right hand out for Gabriel to assist him through the window. Gabriel's hand embraced Ray's as he hoisted himself through the window. Before he could completely make it through, A slight scraping sound began echoing through the empty hallway. "Oh shit, what the hell was that?" Gabriel asked. Ray shook his head in frustration "I reckon that is an indication that our barricade ain't going to last much longer." Ray said as he finished assisting Gabriel through the window and picked up two of the bottles off of the roof, making his way to the middle part of it. This, in turn, gave him a little distance between himself and the other two men. Now feeling comfortable with the roof's stability, Gabriel stationed himself on the left corner of it.

With his revolvers fully loaded, Mavrick picked up one of the bottles while warning Ray and Gabriel. "Old Red seems to be okay guys, and these undead bastards seem to be leaving him alone. Be careful when shooting the bottles though, if we shoot too late or hit it while it's too high in the air, we may kill our ride out of here. The last thing we need is to be down another horse." Mavrick then drew the bottle in his right hand back and tossed it into the air like a tomahawk. While spinning through the air, he drew his revolver, hitting the bottle with a bullet. This caused the bottle to shatter into a million tiny pieces and combust into a giant blanket of fire. As the combination of glass and fire descended upon the rotting flesh, the creatures became engulfed in the fire faster than dried out, decomposing leaves. Ray and Gabriel then threw their first bottles and fired, following suit with Mavrick. Ray shattered it with his first shot, covering the creatures below in a sea of fire.

Gabriel, unfortunately, missed the first one but made contact with the second bullet.

    At this point, the men were looking down at what looked like a small forest of fire. The wind started picking up, causing the top layer of the flames to flutter wildly, allowing the hottest part of the flame to reach over to other zombies. This caused them to ignite in a similar fashion of a wick on a candle being lit by a match. Mavrick picked up his second bottle and slipped in his satchel while instructing Ray and Gabriel to hand him theirs. Gabriel's eyebrows scrunched up, and his jaw dropped, "Why would we stop? Those undead bastards are coming ablaze, ain't that what we want?" Ray intervened, "yeah, but look how quickly the fire is spreading." Gabriel took a moment to really take in what was going on around him. The fire was now moving so fast it spread to two zombies every couple of seconds. It was so big at this point, and the zombies were so close together to the men it looked like a sea of fire. Mavrick's face clenched, and his eyes widened, displaying how worried he actually was. "Guys, this fire is getting way out of control. It is spreading much faster than I initially thought, and if it continues going down the route, we may not be able to stay here much longer." Ray asked, "What do you mean?"

Mavrick pointed down at the zombies directly at the stairs headed on the porch. "With how quickly these undead creatures are catching on fire and how close they are to one another; I would say we will be lucky if the house doesn't catch ablaze soon." Ray then pointed to where the first blanket of fire fell upon the undead and said, "Well, at least they seem to be taking effect." Suddenly there was a sound of heavy wood slamming on the floor behind them down the hall. "Ohhh shit," Gabriel muttered through a slight gasp as he turned toward the window to see what was going on. "Ray, Mavrick, I don't know if you heard any of that, but we need to get out of here now!" Gabriel was as pale as a ghost at this point and sweating profusely. Ray looked through the sea of fire and decay, seeing his horse Red still hitched to one of the posts. The horse was frantic but didn't seem to have any apparent injuries.

"Mavrick, Gabriel is right; we need to make our way out of here." Ray pointed into the window that was behind them with his right hand. "It sounds like a group of those bastards were strong enough to knock over the barricade we set up." Ray put his hand down and drew his revolvers, turning toward the window and firing in through it. Mavrick smirked a little as his eyes lit up, and he pointed down to where the first blanket of fire fell upon the hoard, seeing their lifeless bodies collapse to the ground. "The plan is working guys, all we need to do is hold out a few more moments, and we should be able to get the hell out of here." Ray continued open firing into the hall, "That's great, but please tell me that moment is going to be coming soon because I ain't going to be able to hold these freaks off for long." Mavrick nodded, acknowledging his concern, "Gabriel, give Ray a hand. Listen closely, because when I say go, we are going to jump down and make a run for Red."

Gabriel stepped up toward the window as Ray emptied his rounds and started reloading. The undead creatures began making strides against the barrage of bullets. Before they could make it too far, Ray finished loading up the revolvers and joined back in the bullet storm that he and Gabriel were a part of. One headshot after another, the corpses fell, and they successfully pushed back the hoard back, buying themselves a little time. A strong gust of wind from the northwest caught the essence of the fire, passing it like a baton to the zombies on the porch. The smoke began rising around the ledges of the porches, blocking their view of the men's escape route. Mavrick started squinting due to a combination of an attempt to keep his focus on the path he had planned and the consistent burning from the smoke. The wood roof that the three men were standing on started to produce a dark grey cloud of smoke. Ray covered his mouth with his right sleeve attempting to keep out as much of the smoke out of the fear it may invoke another coughing fit.

    Within moments the cloud of smoke transformed into a massive wall of fire, separating Mavrick from the other two men. "Shit!" Gabriel said, instinctually throwing his arms up to shield his eyes as the fire continued to flare up. Mavrick started yelling through the flames, "Guys, get ready!". Gabriel and Ray noticed that the smoke began to fill the hall from the stairwell as they nodded toward each other, yelling back to Mavrick, "Ready!". The smoke now completely concealed the undead hoard that inhabited the home as both Gabriel and Ray turned around toward the street. All three men were trying to put themselves into the right state of mind for what they were about to endure. "Go!" Mavrick's voice echoed back to the two men as it followed him into the horde of the undead creatures. Ray and Gabriel both leaped down as the roof all three men were just standing on collapsed in on itself, and it became completely engulfed in flames.

Thanks to the momentum, Ray ended up falling into a roll, only doing it one time and then coming back up into a run. As Gabriel made contact with the ground, he started to trip. Still, he regained his momentum until he was stabilized and continued to run through a burning pack of creatures. All three men had their arms up, protecting their faces as they continued to push the zombies out of the way. Once they made it about halfway through the yard, every step they took forward taxed their perception of time. This made it feel as if they were going to be trapped there forever and consumed by the sea of burning zombies. Somehow Ray was the first one to make it out, running until he passed the wooden fence posts. He ran over to Old Red and attempted to unhitch him quickly. Before he could ultimately get the reins untied, two of the Zombies reached their burning, decomposing claws out, trying to get a grip on Ray. Their claws looked like an oddly shaped torch at this point, as they were mere inches from Ray's face. Before either of the undead creatures could make any more progress, they fell backward among their fellow-creatures and their bodies started convulsing as well as a decaying body could.

Ray finished unhitching old red then mounted his trusty steed while Gabriel and Mavrick departed the hoard. Ray rode Old Red over to where Gabriel was standing, reached out his hand, and yelled for him to "get on!" After a slight moment of hesitation, Gabriel nodded while grabbing Ray's hand and pulling himself up on the back of the horse. Even though Red was a decent-sized horse, there was no way that he would have been able to carry all three men. So before Ray made his way to Mavrick's location, he yelled for them to go ahead and that he would meet up with the two of them at the saloon. "Which saloon?" Gabriel asked while running his left hand through his hair and his right hand held his hat. Mavrick seemed puzzled; how many saloons are there?" Gabriel paused for a moment, looking around wildly. "I believe that there are only two; the one on this side of town is called the Lucky Spade Saloon, while the one on the other side of town is called Jack Eye's Saloon."

Ray looked around the yard, every inch now completely covered with the burning corpses, none of which showed even a sign of being reanimated. In the center of the yard, the old house was now completely engulfed in the hot flames. Ray proceeded to chime in, "Let's meet at Jack Eye's Saloon in a few hours." Mavrick nodded and then proceeded to run off in the other direction while Ray turned Old Red around, and the two men followed the road back into town. This time not only did they leave a trail of dust behind them, but also the charred remains of an old estate, along with the putrid smell of the burnt decaying flesh. The flaring fire continued adding to the horrid smell that would last for ages, much like this memory would last for the three of them involved.

Chapter 13 Witch Hunt

When Old Red made it to his destination, Ray and Gabriel slid off the horse. Ray then made his way to the front and hitched his horse up to one of the horse hitches outside the saloon. The saloon was a wooden building composed of a bunch of old planks. Due to the extreme humidity from the environment in which it stood, it started to warp and stray from how it used to look. Not only were a little less than half of the boards bending outwards, but it looked as if the wooden planks, which made up the floor of the porch, were starting to come up. Along with this, only one of the swinging doors that had previously been used to separate the establishment's interior still properly hung there. Its counterpart, on the other hand, had begun to sag down; it looked as if it was being held up barely by a single bolt.

The entrance reached a point of decay that the floorboards became filled with multiple holes, and each one shook when any weight was placed anywhere. Once Old Red was secured to the post, Ray and Gabriel walked up the three old stairs, leading up to the patio and through the doorway. Every step they took was meant with the sound of wood creaking and bending. Ray was hesitant to go any further, as he feared that he would be one step closer to falling through the decomposing wood with each step. After a few moments of hesitation, Ray took a deep breath and continued forward through the doorway while Gabriel followed, staying no more than a few steps behind him. The inside of the saloon was also in poor condition; the state of decay was excessive and overran the building.

Ray noticed every two to three floorboards looked like mice had gnawed through them due to a massive number of holes that were scattered all over the place. An old worn down, black grandmaster piano was placed against the wall to the left where the two men waltzed in. Something peculiar they realized about the piano was that it looked as if it sat crooked. After doing a little more analysis, Ray determined that this was caused by the far-right front leg sinking into one of the holes that made up the odd pattern on the floor. In the middle part of the wall, along the back, was a bar where the only other person in the establishment stood. The guy behind the bar was a buff, tough-looking guy, which both Ray and Gabriel assumed to be the barkeep. This was a bald man with a massive handlebar mustache, indicating he used to have dark brown hair. From an attire standpoint, the barkeep was wearing a long sleeve black button-up shirt with a black tie to match. The Barkeep seemed friendly enough; however, Ray still couldn't help but feel a little uneasy due to the atmosphere and the lack of patrons.

    Gabriel and Ray made their way to the bar, and a man with a smile on his face greeted them. "What can I do for you folks tonight?" he asked. Ray and Gabriel sat down on two empty stools while Ray silently pondered for a moment. "My friend and I would each like a glass of bourbon." The bartender nodded, reinforcing Ray's choice by stating, "Got to say, you have good taste my, friend.". Ray smirked a little, letting out a little chuckle, "Thanks, honestly, that is the nicest thing I heard all day." The barkeep turned around for a moment, shuffling around with the glasses and the drinks. Ray looked over toward Gabriel; taking his hat off his head, he placed it on the bar counter. "So tell me, where do we find this lady you were telling me about, you know, that one that was bad news?"

    Gabriel let out a massive gasp, "You're kidding me! You want to find her? Trust me, Ray, we need to leave and get as far away as possible while we still can. If we don't, she will be the end of us!" It was easy to tell that Gabriel was scared of her, as just a thought caused him to tremble, "Why can't we just get the hell out of dodge while we still got a chance?". Ray shook his head. "No, we need to take care of this now. If we don't, this witch may be persistent, which could be a real issue going forward. Gabriel nodded slightly; the look of hesitation filled his face. The Barkeep turned around, holding two empty glasses in one hand by the rims and a bottle of scotch by the neck in the other. He took turns placing both of the glasses down, one in front of Ray and one in front of Gabriel. Following that, he twisted off the top of the bottle, opened it up, and then tilted it a few inches above the first glass. This allowed the dark brown liquid to fill up about three-fourths of the glass. Ray thanked him as he shuffled around in his satchel. "Not a problem." The barkeep cheerfully said with his smile hiding behind his thick handlebar mustache as he continued pouring into Gabriel's glass. Ray pulled some money out of his satchel, placing it on the bar.

The barkeep scooped up the cash, taking it and placing it in the register once he finished topping off Gabriel's glass. The one door swung open as Mavrick walked in toward the two men. The sound of the door creaking joined the sound of the barkeep shuffling around.

Finally making his way to where the other two men were sitting, Mavrick sat down on the left side of Ray and asked both Gabriel and him what they were having. Ray picked his glass off of the bar, shaking it around, allowing the ice cubes to swirl around like two ships in a terrible cyclone. "Both of us are enjoying the scotch." The barkeep's attention turned toward Mavrick as he asked him with a smile, "what are you having?" Mavrick just pointed at Ray's glass and said, "I'll take what they are having." The barkeep nodded, turning around to grab another glass and the bottle. He turned toward the men and filled Mavrick's drink with the same concoction that filled the other men's glasses.

"So, what's the plan, guys?" Mavrick asked, looking toward the other two men. Ray's eye looked back out of the side under his hat. "Honestly, I ain't really sure. I told Gabriel that we definitely needed to find that witch and stop her in her tracks. If we don't, she may try to attack us again." Before he could say anything else, Ray became overwhelmed with the starting of another coughing fit. Mavrick nodded, "You're right, Ray. But we also need to keep in mind that your health seems to be declining rapidly, so if we are going to find her, we need to do it soon. If we don't, we may never find this Fowler guy." Ray's coughing fit subsided, so while he was catching his breath, he nodded and rubbed his blood-covered hand off on his pants leg. "You're right, Mavrick, so how can we find her as fast as possible?" Mavrick took out some of the money from his satchel and placed it on the bar. The barkeep then grabbed cash, thanking Mavrick. He politely nodded and continued," Actually when before coming here, I ended up bumping into a hooded figure running through the streets. The thing that made it really weird was that the figure kept looking over their shoulder as if they were up to no good." Mavrick placed the rim of the glass to his lips, allowing the booze to pass through, as he continued with what he was saying. "I would have been here sooner, but that person was so suspicious that I couldn't help but follow them and try to figure out if they had any information we could use. "

    Ray placed his cold glass up to his lips, allowing a little bit of the cold liquid to trim the taste buds on his tongue and then to slide down the back of his throat. He nodded his head slightly in acknowledgment of what Mavrick was saying. On the other hand, Gabriel was just staring at Mavrick intently as he continued his story. "The figure hopped on a horse and ended up heading out of town, into the swamps on the northern part of town. I tried to keep up with them, but on horseback, they were just too fast." Mavrick placed his drink up to his lips, allowing himself to take another swig. Ray used this as a moment to chime in. "Didn't that Geneviéve lady say she lived on the outskirts on the northern side of town? Is there anything else that was peculiar about the figure Mavrick?" Mavrick thought for a moment. "Honestly, it was so dark; the only thing I'm really certain of is what I told you. Based on how they were acting, that person has to have something they are hiding."

Ray nodded as he ran his fingers through his beard. "I think we should head north and try to locate this cabin that she was telling me about. I have a feeling it won't be too far up there. Mavrick and Gabriel nodded in agreeance as Mavrick chimed in, "Yeah, all things considered, I would say that is a good idea." The three men put the cold glasses to their lips and threw them back, allowing the remainder of the cold liquid to slide down their throats. The only thing left in the glasses was the remaining ice and what little bit of water originated from the melted ice. The men placed their glasses on the bar in front of them and then stood up. After thanking the barkeep for the service, the three of them made their way to where Old Red was hitched. Ray made his way to the front of Old Red, working on unhitching him while

Mavrick and Gabriel made their way to the horse's right side. "All right, guys. Here is the plan." Rays said, looking in their direction while continuing to unhitch his horse. "Gabriel, you are going to be on Old Red with me. Mavrick, we are going to go at a slow enough pace where you shouldn't have any issues keeping up with us."

Mavrick and Gabriel nodded in agreement as Ray made his way to the opposite side of the horse and then mounted it. Once secured, Ray extended his reach down to Gabriel, offering assistance to get onto the horse. Gabriel accepted, grabbing ahold of Ray's forearm and utilizing it to help stabilize himself while Ray pulled him up. Ray then pulled the reins of Old Red, directing him away from the hitching post and instead toward the road that headed north toward the outskirts of town. Ray ensured that the horse wouldn't go much faster than a trot, which was perfect as it allowed Mavrick to keep up with ease.

After what had to have been about fifty minutes, the men stumbled across a relatively eerie-looking cabin that blended in with the musty old swamp which surrounded it. The cabin looked as if it were constructed with many old wooden planks. The wood looked like it was rotting due to a combination of termites and excessive humidity. This was suggested by a million tiny holes that filled each wooden plank and the extreme warping in the wood. Something else that seemed odd was that this home had windchimes that looked as if they were made from chicken bones. In conjunction with that, a strange symbol was painted in a dark red color, which greatly resembled blood on the front door. Ray let out a sigh of relief "Alright boys, this has to be it." Gabriel let a chuckle out under his breath, "What makes you think that?" Mavrick joined in with a slight smirk on his face, "My guess is the wind chimes." Ray scoffed, "All right, smart asses, I don't need comments from the peanut gallery. All kidding aside, we need to be extra careful going in here as I feel as if we don't really know what she is capable of."

Mavrick nodded as he commented, "There ain't no way this witch is going to provoke us like this and not have some form of defense for her home; that would be stupid." Ray tightened his grip around Old Red's Reigns, throwing his left leg over to the right side of his horse, allowing himself to slide to the ground on the right side of his horse. When his feet hit the ground, both boots splattered in the mud, sending it every which way, in a similar fashion to a rock hitting the water. Ray then handed the reins to Mavrick, instructing him to keep a tight grip on them and ensure nothing happened to Old Red. After accepting Mavrick's nodding as a form of agreement, he continued explaining the plan. "I'm going to go around the house and see if I can find a way in." Mavrick wrapped the reins around his hands, freeing up Ray's and allowing him to cautiously make his way into the old home. With each step, Ray could feel his heart higher and higher in his throat. It felt so high up there at one point he could have sworn that he was about to throw it up.

Once Ray made it to the old wooden steps, he slightly pressed his left boot down on the first stair, with the intent of not placing a lot of pressure just in case of any traps. Noticing nothing was happening, he decided to apply all of his force. No traps were triggered that he was aware of, and Ray let out a sigh of relief as he slowly ascended the rest of the stairs. After what felt like ages, he finally made it onto the porch. And then walked lightly toward the wall, pressing his body against it, slowly moving along it until he was right next to the closest window. Examining it, he realized there was some form of cloth draping over the window preventing him from looking inside. Ray then walked swiftly but quietly until he could reach the window on the left of the door. This window was also completely blocked off with what looked like some kind of blanket. "Shit, are all of these windows going to be covered like this?" Ray asked himself as he tread lightly to the window on the edge of the porch. Even with it being a similar distance to the door, it felt as if it were miles away.

Upon reaching his destination, Ray placed his face up to this glass window to see if he could see anything into this window. "You got to be kidding me," he whispered to himself upon the realization that this window was covered like its counterparts. In a similar fashion as the other windows, there seemed to be a cloth-like material blocking the view. Ray thought about going all the way around the house for a moment, but from what he remembered, the back end of the yard seemed to dip down into the murky water, which became swampland. Feeling the risk of going that way may prove to be far more harmful than productive, Ray made his way back over to the door. Once next to it, he placed his ear against the door as he attempted to pick up on any sound from the inside.

After a few seconds, Ray was able to pick up on some mumbling. However, he found it extremely difficult to make out what was being said. Ray then turned around, slowly making his way toward the top stair of the porch. The top plank let out a soft creek as his body weight pressed down on it. After he hesitated for a moment to ensure whoever was inside didn't respond, he whispered to Gabriel and Mavrick. "All right boys, I ain't sure if it's her, but someone is definitely inside. I think I am going to try knocking and confronting them head-on. I need you guys to be ready, just in case anything goes south."

Both men nodded as they each drew out their revolvers. Ray then instructed them, "Please get out of sight and stay back unless I need you. If this is the same person that was responsible for the incident at the house, the last thing we are going to want to do is to make them feel threatened." Gabriel's face became red as he whispered back at Ray sort of loudly. "You have to be kidding us; I already told you that we should just get the hell out of here. There is no way I'm letting you do this by yourself. Ray raised both hands, keeping the palms down and slowly lowering them, indicating to Gabriel that he needed to calm down. "Look, I'm not suggesting doing this by myself. Just give me some time, and I will call you if I need you. I understand that she has a lot to deal with Gabriel, but with everything I've dealt with over the past few years, she is at the bottom of my list of concerns. Trust me." Gabriel hesitated for a moment, the red disappearing from his face.

Both men nodded again, acknowledging Ray's request as Mavrick secured his grip on Old Red's reigns. He then directed him to some bushes across the muddy road from the old wooden structure. Once in a position where he felt the horse was hidden well enough, he tied his reins around one of the bigger branches that were closer to the base of one that was closer to Old Red's face. Mavrick then crouched down next to Gabriel and Red, utilizing the leaves and the darkness to conceal them. Ray then turned around toward the door and took in a deep breath. Letting out a sigh, he knocked on the door. A woman's voice came through, substantially muffled. Ray assumed that this had to be due to the door being constructed of solid wood. "Who's there?" due to her accent being thick in conjunction with the sound being muffled, he could barely make out what she was saying. Ray cleared his throat so that he would be able to speak clearly, "My name is Ray. I just want to talk for a moment." Void of any response, Ray placed his ear to the door and was able to pick up on some shuffling from inside. Suddenly it became quiet, then without any warning, the sound of multiple mechanisms could be heard in the door itself.

Ray quickly pushed himself away from the door and waited for the woman on the inside to finish unlocking what sounded like ten locks; each one had to take two to three seconds to unlock. Once all the locks were finally unlatched, the woman opened the door a little bit so that she could look out the crack. Her right brown eye, along with the caramel-colored skin on her cheek, could be seen through it. "What brings you here, Ray?" The woman's eyes looked him up and down as if checking to see if he had anything on him that she had to worry about. Ray brought a slight smile to his face. "I already told you, I just want to talk. Geneviéve, that's your right?". The woman opened the door all the way and looked frantically to the left and right to ensure that no one followed Ray. She then nodded her head toward the inside of her home, inviting him in. Ray paused and then begrudgingly followed the mysterious woman into the shack.

Once he was in there, Geneviéve pointed to an old, worn chair that sat against the wall at the end of the living room. "Ray, sit down over there; give me a moment, and we will talk." The slight smirk lost all emotion as she turned around and started relocking each of the locks on the door. Ray couldn't help but feel uneasy at this point, not only from the woman locking the door so excessively but also from the atmosphere. The room was poorly lit; what little light filled the room was produced from small candles scattered everywhere through the house. These candles were composed of dark red colored candle wax, which, when melted, could have been easily mistaken for blood.

Another thing that caught Ray's eye was a bookshelf located to the right of where he was sitting. He found it odd that the names of most of the books that sat on the shelves indicated that they had something to do with the Occult. Ray also noticed that to the right of him, through one of the doorways, a room had a glow that seemed to be even dimmer than the room he was currently in. There was something off about that room, and Ray knew if he could get a better look at it, He may better understand what he was dealing with.

Ray leaned his body toward the left a bit in an attempt to see if he could get a glimpse of what the room could have been holding. Geneviéve then stepped in front of him, catching him off guard and causing him to shoot back into sitting up straight. The woman made her way over to a chair directly across from him and took a seat. "How may I be of assistance?" Ray's face was as serious as a heart attack as he began recalling, "Last time we met, you said that if I think of anything, you wanted me to come to see you, right?" Geneviéve's grin slightly emerged on her still face as her eye's stayed stuck to Ray's, watching as a snake does before it strikes.

Her head nodded slowly to confirm his question. Ray continued, "Well, I think I have some information on the band of outlaws." The woman scoffed while glaring at him, "Really? What kind of information do you have?" Ray's facial expression was serious. If looks could kill, his eyes would have been daggers. "Well, for one, I know the name of the gang. I also know who the leader is, which I figured you may want to know." Her eyes widened as her eyebrows raised, and a massive smile came across her face. "Please, Ray, tell me what you know."

Ray hesitated for a moment, silently calculating out his next move. He then abruptly said, "I will; however, there are a few questions I want you to answer for me first." Geneviéve's smile reached an uncomfortable size while she nodded and ran her tongue across the front of her top set of teeth. Her voice projected a sort of mild annoyance. "Well, you are my guest, so please go ahead, ask." Ray started with something that he felt wouldn't escalate the situation "So when we first met, you were asking about this gang of outlaws, you ain't never told me why?" Ray pulled his hat off and placed it on his lap.

Geneviéve then took a deep breath and sighed, "The reason that I am trying to find information on this gang is that my beloved husband Zane died at the hands of those bastards." Her face grew visibly upset as her smile vanished and her eyebrows lowered. "I need to find every last one of those sons of bitches to bring justice to him. That way, he may rest peacefully in the afterlife." Ray started nodding, "I see." He said, his face displayed the empathy he felt for the woman. After all, how could he not? He had also felt the loss of a significant other. He knew the pain of losing the most important person in his life. "If you don't mind me asking, what happened?"

Geneviéve's eyes wandered slightly to the bottom right as she nodded her head slightly. "Zane was a bartender at one of the saloons in town here. He was an honest, hard-working man, trying to make an honest living for us. One night, Zane and I had a marital dispute as I discovered that he walked a young woman home from the bar the night prior. Now he was an honest man, and I knew he was faithful, but it still irked me as he never left the bar until two or three in the morning. Either way, I was irritated with him for the situation, and he got mad at me for getting upset. Unfortunately, he had to work later that evening, and I figured we could make up and talk about everything the next day, so I never had a chance to apologize."

Geneviéve's eyes started to tear up as she cleared her throat in an attempt to prevent interruption of her story. "Later that night, while Zane was running the saloon, a few men made their way into the establishment and pulled a gun out on him. One of his regulars that were there that night later filled me in on what happened. Zane did everything the bastards told him to do and didn't even fight back." Geneviéve started crying hard at this point; tears began streaming down her face. "But one of those bastards decided to shoot him dead like he was some damn animal!"

Ray let out a sigh as he removed his hat and ran his hand through his hair. "I'm terribly sorry for your loss." Geneviéve just nodded, biting her lower lip. "It ain't your fault." her frown became an intense snarl as she wiped away the tears from her face. I am going to find each and every one of those bastards, and they will die!" Ray then asked calmly "how do you plan on doing that?" Geneviéve's display of pain almost wholly left her expression at this point. She started laughing in almost a mocking tone, "Ahhh, Ray, I don't think I can tell you that."

Ray's face continued to hold a grip of complete seriousness; his eyes locked onto hers yet again. "Fine, are you aware of any weird things happening around town here?" Geneviéve's face seemed to match Ray's, displaying her grave feelings. "What do you mean?" Ray answered her question while analyzing her full facial expression in an attempt to find any form of deceit, "Just anything out of the ordinary." he paused for a moment. "You know, like zombies?" Geneviéve's grin came back onto her face, and her head cocked a little to the left. "So Ray, let me ask you a question, what zombies?" Ray started biting his lower lip as his eyebrows scrunched up out of irritation, "I believe you know what I'm talking about." Geneviéve started to laugh, "Are you suggesting that I had something to do with zombies?" The smile quickly fled from her face as it became filled with annoyance, almost as if she was offended.

Ray decided that it would be best to play down his point of view as this woman seemed to be unhinged, "I'm not; I'm just wondering if you may have seen anything odd like I have." Geneviéve's eyes widened as she prompted him, "Go on." Ray continued, "When I was riding through town, I noticed that there was a house that was surrounded by a group of people. I decided that it may be a good idea to check out to ensure everything was okay. Still, when I made it close enough to get a better look, the smell of rotting flesh came over me, and I was aghast. Not only due to the smell, but also due to the sight of decaying corpses walking around."

Geneviéve started nodding as her face went from the offended look to one of more understanding. "I see; I still am trying to figure out why you would think I would know anything about these zombies." She started to glare at Ray once more. "Once again, I'm not saying you do. I just thought with you being in the area, you may have seen something out of the ordinary." Ray's voice was starting to shake at this point out of frustration of having to repeat himself. Geneviéve proceeded to nod again as her glare loosened up, and she was smiling that slightly malicious one that she had prior.

    Ray released a quiet deep breath of relief, thanks to de-escalating Geneviéve from her highly paranoid state. Unfortunately, as much as he wanted to leave, he knew that he still needed to retrieve more information from her. "So Geneviéve, do you know anythi- *cough cough cough* "Ray was caught off guard by another coughing fit. As he attempted to regain his composure and control over his breathing, Geneviéve's smile disappeared as her eyebrows rose. She then asked with a slight look of concern on her face, "You okay, Ray?" As he covered his mouth with his left hand and continued to violently cough into it, he raised his right hand up with his thumb up to indicate that he was fine.

    After a few minutes, his coughing fit finally ceased, and he was hunched over, attempting to catch his breath through deep heaves. Pulling his hand away, he noticed more blood, this time, it almost completely covered the side of his fist. "Shit, I don't have much more time." Ray thought to himself. Geneviéve shook her head a bit as her mouth hung open slightly, attempting to take in what she was seeing. "You ain't okay, are you Ray?" He responded by shaking his head, "Honestly, I ain't sure. Regardless of how I am, I need to find the bastard that did this to me." Geneviéve tilted her head, and her mouth transformed into a slightly twisted smile. "Now, I may be able to help with that, but I want you to promise if I do, you will leave me be." Ray squinted while cocking his head to the side. "Really? How are you going to help me?" She proceeded to laugh, "Simple Voodoo." Ray's eyes widened, "Voodoo?" she continued, "You heard me right. Once my husband passed away, I swore vengeance on the people responsible, and that is when I dedicated my life to voodoo."

    Ray leaned back, crossing his arms as he was processing Geneviéve's story. "A friend of mine who was a high priestess in it consoled me when my husband died, and after seeing what I went through, she offered me a way to avenge him. This friend and I met up three times a week for a year, and she taught me everything she knew about voodoo." Ray nodded, "I see, so how do you suppose you can help me?" Responding so quickly she almost cut Ray off, Geneviéve said, "I would more less act as a channel, so that you may speak with Papa Legba. If you ask him for something, he can assist. But be warned, everything has a price."

Ray's right eyebrow raised out of curiosity, "What do you mean a price? Geneviéve just shrugged. "That's between you and him." Ray thought about it for a moment as he sat quietly, running his left hand through his facial hair. "I am running out of time, and this may be the quickest way to find them. But at what cost?" he mumbled to himself. Geneviéve then asked Ray, "So what will it be?" Ray sighed as he looked away for a moment, then, after a slight hesitation, looked back into her eyes and nodded slowly.

"Good, let us begin then, follow me," Geneviéve said as she started walking through the door that caught Ray's attention earlier. The room was lit up with blood color candles similar to those that lit up the rest of the shack. But there were significantly less than what the rest of the house had. The home also had multiple symbols etched into parts of the floorboards, while other symbols were marked in place with some form of a white powdery substance that resembled chalk.

In the middle of the room, on the floor, laid a black rug in the shape of a circle. It looked big enough for at least six people to sit on the edges and one in the middle. At the end of the room, something looked like an altar. This contained many odd symbols similar to other ones found around the room. Along with those sat a picture of Geneviéve and what Ray assumed to be her husband. It was placed in front of that sat a massive book that laid open. The altar was surrounded by eight candles, which she used as her primary light source when reading the text.

Geneviéve made her way over to the altar and started flipping through the pages of the book. Once she found what she was looking for, she then placed her finger onto the paper, saying, "Here it is." Geneviéve then opened one of the cabinets built into the bottom part of the altar and started rummaging around the contents within it. After about a minute of her moving the stuff in the cabinet around, she pulled out four mason jars. Each one had different words written on them, labeling its contents. The first jar contained sugarcane juice, another had pecans, the third said sugar cookies and the fourth displayed licorice. Geneviéve then placed the jars down on the floor next to the altar and asked Ray, "Would you do me a favor while I finish preparing? I need you to find three coins that have the same denomination?" Ray hesitated for a moment, thinking it was an odd request, but he did it anyway.

    Geneviéve opened a small drawer between the top part of the altar and the cabinet to remove the jars. After a moment of rummaging around in it, she fished out a black candle. She then grabbed one of the red candles, which were lit with her right hand, and brought both to the center of the rug. Geneviéve then utilized the red candle to light the black one and placed both on opposite sides of the carpet. She put the red one toward the north and the black one toward the south of the rug. While this was going on, Ray was rummaging around in his satchel, trying to find the coins he needed. Geneviéve then went back to the small drawer under the altar. She retrieved her black candle and pulled out a pack of cigarettes.

    Geneviéve then rummaged through the cabinet under the altar yet again, pulling out an old bottle full of a clear liquid. Geneviéve then unwrapped the pack, removed two single cigarettes, and placed the box on the altar. Making her way to the circular rug again, she put the two cigarettes just to the left of the center and the rum just shy to the right. Ray held his right hand out in a closed fist, holding what he had been looking for. "Geneviéve, here I found what you needed." Ray reached out his arm with his hand in a fist, concealing something. She smirked as she stuck out her hand, palm up, ready to receive the coins. "Thank you, Ray." Geneviéve then placed the coins in a pile about the same distance from the center as she did with the cigarettes and the rum.

"Okay, now there is one last thing that we need, and then we can get started." Geneviéve said as she untangled something from around her neck. Ray cocked his head a little to the left as he squinted as he asked, "What is it?". "This," Geneviéve said as she grabbed a unique-looking symbol which was the centerpiece of the necklace that she was wearing. She then removed it, placed it in the palm of her hand, and held it out for Ray to see. The only way Ray could describe the symbol was that it looked like a cross with a shape similar to a square in the middle of it. The thing that he found odd was that the strange-looking shape's corners didn't actually connect. Another thing that caught

Ray's eye with this symbol was that there were many unique, highly detailed signs etched into it that he had never seen before.

Ray's face maintained all seriousness. "I'll ask again, what is it?". Geneviéve smirked a bit, "Why must you be so uptight Ray? This is called the Veve of Papa Legba." Ray's eyebrows rose out of confusion "What the hell is a Veve?" Geneviéve answered without a second thought "Think of it as a sacred symbol." She said as she made her way over to the carpet sitting down, with both legs folded in and getting herself into a more comfortable position "You sure that you are ready to meet Papa Legba, Ray? He can be very intimidating." Ray nodded "Yeah I am." Geneviéve's face lost her smirk as she instructed Ray "Okay, then please sit as I sit across from me and I will begin the prayer." Ray followed the woman's instructions, sitting down in a similar manner to her.

Once in position, Geneviéve raised her head toward the sky and recited the following prayer: "Papa Legba, open the gate for me. Antibon Legba please open the gate. Legba open the gate for me, and I will thank the Iwa when I return." Geneviéve then became as silent as the night. At the same time, Ray analyzed his environment, seeing if he could notice any odd changes indicating the prayer was working. The only thing that he could tell had changed was that the room had become so silent one could have heard a pin drop. Doubt started to fill his mind as he asked, "So how does this Papa Legba make himself known?" Before Ray could get a response, both of the lit candles went out almost as if a strong gust of wind hit them, causing the room to become engulfed in darkness. A faint deep voice filled the void darkness behind Ray, saying, "Like this." Ray's eye's widened while his body stiffened as he became almost completely frozen out of fear.

    While it was difficult to see anything, Papa Legba's outline could be made out faintly. It looked as if it was a tall and skinny-looking man. The figure seemed to be cloaked in dark rag-like clothing, which assisted with helping it blend into the shadows. Another thing that caught Ray's attention was that Papa Legba looked like he wore something upon his head that bore a striking resemblance to a straw hat. Somehow, the figure's voice had such a tone that it seemed so calm but intimidating. The voice seemed to float fluidly around the room as the creature's figure seemed to vanish back into the shadows. Ray's eyes jerked around rapidly, shifting through the darkness as he attempted to figure out where Papa Legba had gone. Without so much as a warning, Ray looked to his right and was greeted by two eyes that had a sort of dim, white glow to them. They couldn't have been any farther than a few inches from his face.

    The eyes seemed to stay locked on Ray as they moved above the circular rug, seeming to move back and forth slowly at sort of a pace. Papa Legba began speaking again in a calm tone, "Geneviéve, Ray, why do you summon me? How may I be of assistance?" Geneviéve noticed the intimidation seemed to have caused the cat to catch Ray's tongue. So to prevent upsetting the being, she spoke up, "Papa Legba, the reason we summoned you is that Ray needs your help. Ray, speak with him; he is listening." Ray sort of shook his head to combat the shock that he was trapped in. "Right, Papa Legba, it is I that humbly asks for your assistance." The figure proceeded to laugh. A slight growl could be heard under each chuckle. " Okay, what do you need from me?" Ray cleared his throat in an attempt to prevent his voice from shaking. "The reason we have summoned you is that I need to find the person that gave me this disease. There is a girl that he and his gang kidnapped and are holding captive. I fear if I don't get to her soon, it's going to be too late, and that bastard is going to do this to someone else."

Papa Legba continued pacing around the carpet, "I see, and how exactly do you expect me to help? I am not known for tracking." He ceased movement in the middle of the carpet at that moment, keeping his eyes locked on Ray. "I am the gatekeeper to the other world." Geneviéve jumped in, "Papa Legba, you have always been good to me after the death of my husband. It was I that recommended we reach out to you, as you have always assisted me." The eye's vanished as Papa Legba's voice now came from behind Geneviéve "Tis true; however you have been a practitioner for a while, us Loa see favor upon you." He paused for a moment as his voice suddenly appeared behind Ray again. "For my assistance, Ray. What would you offer me?"

Ray thought for a moment as he rubbed his hand through his beard. "What are you looking for?" Papa Legba continued, "Well, as you can imagine, I have all I need. Your service, however, may prove to be of value, and one cannot put a price on loyalty." Ray paused for a moment as his eyes widened, "What? What do you mean?" Papa Legba started to laugh again, this time slightly louder than prior.

"Simple, going forward, I may have requests for you. If I ask you for something, do it. No matter my request."

The hair on the back of his neck began sticking up. "What kind of stuff would I be doing?" Papa Legba was directly in front of Ray at this point. His dim white eyes glared at him as his voice became sterner. "Ray, I am starting to lose my patience. I reassure you that you will be able to handle anything that I ask of you. Quickly now, do you accept my help? Yes, or no?" After a brief moment of hesitation, Ray gave his answer. "Yeah." Papa Legba started pacing the rug at this point. "Very good, you are a wise man, Mr. Williams." he said as he began to chuckle that laugh that contained that deep growl. Papa Legba then made his way back to the front of Ray and this time looked as if he had crouched down to meet Ray at his current height. His dimly glowing eyes stared back into Ray's. "Do you have the pocket watch on you, Ray?" He nodded, his eyebrows raised, displaying the shock that overcame him. "Yeah, I do. How'd you know?" Papa Legba laughed again, "Well boy, the other spirits tell me all, take it out, let me see it." Ray rummaged around in the satchel for a moment to find the pocket watch. He then pulled it out and handed it to Papa Legba.

The watch would have looked like it was floating by itself if it weren't for the outline of the loa's hand holding it. Suddenly, the watch seemed to vanish almost entirely in a cloud of smoke that filled the air. The only thing that could still be seen was the chain swinging back and forth at a relatively steady pace. "Ray, place your hand out, palm up." Papa Legba instructed. Ray followed suit, placing his right hand's open palm face up, and in return, Loa placed the watch down in it. "Okay, Ray. It is done." Ray turned his head slightly to the right as he scrunched up his eyebrows in confusion, "What's done?"

Papa Legba began to chuckle again. "I modified your watch for you to show you the way. The minute and hour hands will continue to work as normal, but when you grip the watch tightly and tell the spirits what you're looking for, it will point you in the direction that you need to go." Ray nodded slowly. "I see." he said, "Thanks again, Papa Legba." The loa continued, "Ray, you must be cautious when using the watch. The way it works is multiple spirits will communicate with one another to pick up on the direction you need to go. Once they figure out what they need to know, they will adjust the second hand accordingly, guiding you in the direction that you need to go. It will act almost like a compass, except rather than guiding you toward the north, it will guide you toward your desires. Remember, the watch will act as a beacon to any spirit, both good and evil. Not only will it show them where you are headed but also where you are."

Ray asked, "Is this even safe?". Papa Legba responded, "In moderation, you should be okay. Just make sure that you are prepared to fight before using it. The spirits it is meant to work with are those of the dead and the other loa of Voodoo. But Ray, many creatures are spiritual entities, and some of these are evil such as demons. When you use this, you may have a target on your back." Papa Legba made his way back to the outside of the circular rug and proceeded to start walking around the two of them as he asked, "Geneviéve, Ray is there anything else Papa Legba can do for you?" Geneviéve and Ray both remained silent as they shook their heads no. The Loa then disappeared with his distinct laugh, and the candles lit back up automatically. Geneviéve then stood back up to her feet, and Ray followed.

Geneviéve had a smirk on her face and asked Ray, "Is there anything else that I could be of assistance with?" Ray hesitated for a moment, contemplating his next move. "Actually, yes." Geneviéve's eyes widened as she was caught off guard by Ray's response. "Please, bear with me as I explain. There is a man named Gabriel. He was part of the gang that murdered your husband. However, he didn't kill him." Geneviéve's face turned red as she was becoming visibly upset. Ray continued, "Geneviéve, I am going to need him when I confront this bastard that did this to me. If you can spare him, just him, I vow that when this is over, I will assist you in hunting down the rest of those bastards that did that to your husband." Geneviéve's face was grave at that point; it radiated the extreme emotions of anger and pain. After a brief moment of silence, she nodded slowly. "Fine, I will let him live, but he will not go unpunished; even though it may not be my hand that strikes him, the Loa always seeks justice. But Ray, if you make it through this, I expect you to keep your word."

Ray nodded "I am nothing if I ain't a man of my word." Ray said as he stuck his hand out with his palm open, offering to shake her hand. She reached her hand out and meant his as they shook their hands. Geneviéve then led Ray to the door, again thanking her for her assistance. She then made her way back into the home as Ray made his way over to where Mavrick and Gabriel were waiting. He was greeted by Mavrick petting Old Red and Gabriel with a Furious look on his face, "What happened? Why the hell did you let her live! I told you she is a danger to us!"

    Mavrick just continued petting the horse as if trying to maintain his distance from this conversation. Ray defended his decision "It's simple Gabriel, the fact of the matter is that she is the way she is because she is a victim. After explaining the situation to her and gaining her trust, we came to an arrangement." Gabriel started laughing out of disbelief, "Ray, she cannot be trusted; she is a damn witch!" Without turning around, Mavrick defended Ray. "Honestly, Gabriel, I haven't known Ray for long, but I'm sure he wouldn't make a call like this lightly." Gabriel blurted out once again, his tongue was sharp and his temper hot, "You're making a damn fool out of yourself! She is going to betray-" Ray put his hand up, stopping Gabriel in his tracks. "Listen, I understand why you don't trust her, but please, if you don't do anything else, trust me. Even if anything goes south, I will do everything in my power to make sure we are okay. If she tries anything, we will track her down again and put an end to her. But as of now, it is unlikely that she will do anything because having us on her side is far more beneficial for her."

Gabriel threw his hands in the air like a child throwing a tantrum. "Fine, but if this backfires, Ray, don't say I didn't warn you." Mavrick finally turned away from the horse and faced both of the men, "So guys, what's that plan?" Ray pulled the pocket watch out of the satchel, dangled it from the chain, and allowed it to swing back and forth, slowly in front of the two other men, "We are going to use this to track down the son of a bitch that did this to me. We are going to save the shopkeeper's daughter and prevent this from happening to anyone else." Mavrick nodded "that sounds like a plan boss. If possible, we should stop for the night and get some rest. It's pretty late after all." Ray nodded in agreement, "Gabriel, I know I didn't handle this situation exactly how you wanted me to, but please stick with us and give us a hand with tracking down this guy. It will be the perfect opportunity to get you out of the life of crime and make a positive difference somehow. Without hesitation, Gabriel nodded "I will help you guys, mainly because I'm tired of being a part of this. I'm tired of causing pain. Besides, I've been tempting fate way too long. If I keep going the way I am going, I'm gonna end up with a damn noose around my neck. Ray stuck his hand out toward Gabriel, offering to embrace him in a handshake as a slight smirk came to his face. "Thanks, Gabriel. I really appreciate it, my friend." Gabriel obliged, firmly gripping Ray's hand, and the two men shook hands.

Ray then looked over the pocket watch, opened it, and laid it flat in his open palm. He hesitated for a moment and then gripped the sides while saying, "I am looking for Travis Anthony Fowler." The second hand started spinning wildly in every direction, so much so that it may make its way entirely around ten times within a second. After about ten seconds, it stopped on a dime facing the north. Blown away that Papa Legba's assistance was actually working; Ray couldn't help but change the direction he was facing to see if that had any effect on the second hand. Of course, Papa Legba's voodoo worked as planned; even the slightest movement was mirrored by the second hand. "Wow, this is crazy!" Ray mumbled to himself, blown away that Papa Legba could do something like this. After the astonishment wore off, Ray began letting Mavrick and Gabriel in on his plan. "We are going to need to head north, but before we go, It may not be a bad idea to grab a horse for you two. After all, we don't know how far away we are going to be traveling." Gabriel then stepped toward a bit. "There are a few horses at the hideout that the branch of the gang I was a part of uses. It's actually right on the outskirts of town, so we may be able to swing by and snatch two horses without anyone knowing." Ray had a hesitant look in his eye, clearly uneasy about the idea. How wouldn't he be, they had dealt with enough trouble going on to keep them busy for days, and Ray's condition just continued to get worse.

    Mavrick chimed in, "Ray, I understand why you're hesitant, but you are right; we do need a few horses. Honestly, I think this will be the most efficient way. It may take a little time to snatch them, however when it comes to the trip itself, it may make everything much more efficient." Ray, clearly still hesitating, nodded slowly, "I know, I was just hoping there would've been an easier way to get them. You know, preferably a way that wouldn't place such a big target on our backs." Gabriel nodded, saying, "Don't worry, Ray. Like I said, the gang's hideout isn't far, and they still think that I'm one of them. So, we just need to make our way to the horses, which are located in the outer part of the hideout, inside the barn. Once there, Mavrick and I can snatch two horses, and we should be out of there in no time." Ray walked over to Old Red, pulling himself up onto his horse "Okay, Gabriel, lead the way." Gabriel followed the road back into town with a nod while Ray and Mavrick followed him.

    Once surrounded by the massive buildings, the men got off the main road and started venturing through the smaller streets. Eventually, they made it to a small alleyway that had a gate blocking off the entrance, "This is it." Gabriel said as he walked up to it. Mavrick chuckled, "You're telling me that this is your hideout?" Gabriel turned around and pulled the gate open, allowing the two other men entry. "Yeah, actually, the buildings are all interlocked, so if we ever needed to stand our ground, it allows us to redistribute members to other parts of the hideout. This, in turn, makes us better prepared for gunfights, now quiet down, I don't believe there is anyone in the barn, but still, it is better to not draw attention." Ray got off Old Red and hitched him just outside of the gate. Once secured, Mavrick and Ray made their way through it, and Gabriel followed them, leaving the gate open. Once all three men were on the other side of the gate, Gabriel led them to another building with massive doors that were direct to the right of them. The door was painted a dark brown color and looked as if it would be heavy. This proved to be deceiving as when

Gabriel pulled it open, it didn't take much effort on his part, and it opened in a pretty fluid motion.

Gabriel made his way into the big stables, while Mavrick followed him. Ray stayed just a few steps back to keep an eye out for any trouble. Making their way to the back half of the Stables, Gabriel led Mavrick over to a black quarter horse on the left side of the stables. "Take this one, Mavrick. I'm going to grab another," Gabriel said as he made his way into a pin on the right side of the stables that held a white quarter horse. Gabriel grabbed a saddle hanging on the opening part of the gate. He then placed it on the horse and secured it with the straps. Gabriel then put the Reins around its mouth. Even though it was going pretty smooth and taking a few minutes, the gravity of the situation made the situation feel like it was hours. Gabriel opened the gate, led the horse out of the pin, and made his way back to Mavrick. Ensure that it was easy for him to get out and ensure that he had the most straightforward path possible. By the time he made it there, the black quarter horse was wholly geared up. Gabriel made his way over to the gate of the pin and opened it up for Mavrick as he pulled himself onto the back of the horse. As Mavrick and the black quarter horse started making their way out of the gate, Gabriel pulled himself onto the white one. As both men headed out toward the way they entered, Mavrick rode up to Ray. He then reached his hand out, offering Ray assistance to get on the horse. Ray accepted, grabbing hold of Mavrick's forearm, and then he pulled Ray up with all of his might. Ray kicked his leg over the horse and landed on the back of the saddle in one fell swoop.

With all three men saddled up, they started making their way out of the stables. The men ensured to keep the horse at a trot to keep the noise down and decrease the odds of getting caught. Suddenly two men wearing black cowboy hats and long black dusters blocked the door, each holding a peacemaker at the ready. "What the hell are you doing, Gabriel, and who are these half-wits?" The tension became so high one could hear a pin drop. Gabriel was so caught off guard his voice was trembling even though his nervous laugh. "Oh, these folks are um," he hesitated for a moment, "new recruits, the boss told me to take them out and show them how we work."

The man on the right was squinting hard, his eyebrows scrunched up as he glared at Gabriel, "Funny, the boss didn't tell me about new recruits. Speaking of which, where is Rick? Wasn't he with you?" Gabriel nodded slowly, his mouth and his eyes wide open, "Yeah, he was. We ran into town, but when we finished what we were doing, he told me that he had some other errands to run and that he would meet up with me later." The man on the left then chimed in, "Gabriel, didn't you have a horse when you went out with Rick? Why do you need another one?" Gabriel let out a slight chuckle. "Actually, Tim, I rode with Rick so that we didn't have to each have a horse, we figured it would be easier that way, and unfortunately, when he took off, he took the horse with him." The guy on the left looked to the one on the right, and both of them simultaneously put their revolvers down. They then stepped to the sides of the doors while the one on the right apologized. "Sorry for the inconvenience, friends. You just can't be too careful nowadays. Gabriel nodded in agreement with them, "No, you are right, I completely understand. You gentlemen have a wonderful night.".

Ray, Mavrick, and Gabriel rode past the men on their horses. They trotted back toward the opening where they initially entered the alleyway. While they made their way through the opening, the heavy stable doors could be heard being closed by the two men they ran into. After a few moments, they finally made it to the opening of the alleyway, and Ray slid off of Mavrick's horse and headed over to Old Red, unhitching him. He then made his way over to Old Red's side and pulled himself upon his back while Mavrick let out a breath of relief. Mavrick removed his hat as he ran his fingers through his hairs" Well, that was a close one, guys. Ray, do you have any idea what the next step is?"

    Ray got himself balanced and sat in a comfortable position on top of his horse. He shuffled through his satchel for a moment; removing the old pocket watch, he opened it up and placed it back into the open palm of his hand. He then wrapped his fingers around the sides, saying, "I am looking for Travis Anthony Fowler." Ray watched for a moment as the second hand spun wildly out of control, and then, much like before, it stopped pointing north. Ray looked up from the watch toward Mavrick, "The plan remains as it was before; we need to go north. I'm not sure how far, but why don't we make our way out of the city and then get some sleep. After all, it is getting late, and we could use some rest with everything we just dealt with." Mavrick and Gabriel nodded in agreement and followed Ray on horseback onto the main road through the city. They continued north as the road guided them back outside of Saint Edgerton.

Chapter 14 Ghouls and Nightmares

After riding for about an hour, the men found a spot of ground that was dry enough to set up camp. Unfortunately, they didn't have any camping supplies due to previous events. Gabriel slid off his horse made his way to the edge of where they were planning on camping. He then tied the white quarter horse's reins around the trunk of one of the trees. After tugging on the reins to ensure that his horse was secured, Gabriel made his way into the sea of trees to locate some wood they could use to make a fire. This time, Mavrick decided to stay back with Ray, which both of them seemed a good idea because the consistent moisture in the air seemed to worsen his condition. Ray and Mavrick both slid off their horses, and Mavrick grabbed both their reins. He then led them over to a few trees on the edge of the camp, and he tied them up to the trunks of two different trees. As Mavrick finished up, Gabriel made his way back through the tree line, holding a pile of big sticks and smaller logs. Ray had made his way over to the most open area of the where he deemed would be the safest place to set up a fire. He then waved Gabriel over to where he was standing. "Bring the wood over to me, and I will get it started." Ray said, his voice shaking a bit from exhaustion, "I may be ill, but I can still be useful." Gabriel nodded as he made his way over to Ray, then he gently placed the firewood down at his feet.

Ray then kneeled to one knee and started placing the smaller pieces of wood in shape similar to a wigwam. Once they were in place, he put the larger pieces against them to keep the sticks up. Ray then rummaged through his satchel and located a pack of matches on him. Gabriel came back over, his hands full with a giant pile of leaves. "Here you go, Ray. This should help with getting it lit." Ray reached for the pile, "Thanks." He grabbed the leaves and carefully placed them under the pile of wood. Ray then lit a match and threw it into the middle of his constructed stack. The wind picked up after a few moments, catching the tiny flame. This caused it to flail around violently as it quickly consumed the leaves. With the tip of the fire completely covering the sticks at this point, it wasn't long before they too became consumed. With the fire now going strong, Ray was comfortable that it wouldn't go out. He backed away a few inches and collapsed backward from exhaustion, falling to his butt.

Both Mavrick and Gabriel ran over to check on him. Mavrick asked as he placed his hand on his shoulder. "Ray, you alright?" At this point, Ray was succumbing to his exhaustion, fighting to get out what he was trying to say between deep heavy breaths. "Yeah," *cough cough,* "I'll be okay. I'm just so tired." *cough cough cough,* "I need to rest." Mavrick then patted Ray on the shoulder. "No worries, boss, why don't you rest? Gabriel and I will stay up for a little while and keep on you". Ray slowly laid backward until the back of his head was lying against the ground. Ray then closed his eyes, and everything went black.

When Ray opened his eyes, he was looking at a familiar ceiling. The sun's light reflected off of it, as it had all those mornings prior. He turned his head to his left to see Elaine's silky blond hair falling perfectly to the pillow, much like a waterfall fills the body of water that it flows into. Seeing his beloved, Ray couldn't keep a smile off his face. For whatever reason, he couldn't help to feel like something was off, but he just couldn't figure out what. Ray turned himself around, pushing him off his side up to a sitting position. He then placed his feet off the side of the bed on the cold wooden floor. After taking a moment, Ray put his hands next to himself on the bed and used them to push himself off it. The moment Ray came to a fully standing position, the room became pitch black, and the sun that filled it was replaced by moonlight. At this moment, the fear kicked in immediately and so intensely that he could feel his heart beating violently in his throat.

Ray's eyes were wide open, and he began sweating profusely as he slowly turned around. As soon as Ray was facing back toward the bed, he noticed a dark figure standing over his beloved Elaine. Within seconds went from scared to pissed, "Get away from you, son of a bitch!" he yelled as he began sprinting around the bed in an attempt to save his love. As soon as Ray made it to the corner closest to the figure, it displayed a menacing smile, complemented with two massive obtrusive fangs.

Tears filled Ray's eyes as he sprinted as fast as possible in an attempt to stop this fiend. "I said leave her alone, you bastard!" The creature moved so quickly it was almost like lightning striking as its face descended rapidly upon her. Ray yelled with all of his might, "NO!" He sprinted around the corner of the bed, which was closest to the creature. He attempted to tackle it to the ground without much thought before making any contact with the beast. It disappeared, leaving behind only a disembodied laugh.

Ray then pulled himself off the ground and quickly rushed over toward his sweet Elaine's side. She lay there as she had every night prior. Tears filled his eyes uncontrollably as he looked over her pale body. Ray searched for the slightest hint that there was an ounce of life left in her as he gently slid his hand across her face. He noticed that her skin felt extremely cold to touch, along with two punctures marks where that creature's teeth seemed to be inserted into her neck. He bit his lower lip in an attempt to prevent himself from crying anymore as he leaned over to kiss the lips of his beloved. The only thing that Ray felt was how cold they were. Elaine's eyes opened as he lost his composure and began to weep heavily; Elaine's eyes opened. Her ocean blue eyes that he had gotten lost in time and time again looked down toward him as a smile came to her face. "What are you crying for, Mr. Williams? I always thought you to be a manly man."

Her sweet voice filled his ears as he slowly pulled his head away from her, confused and overwhelmed by disbelief. Elaine smiled that innocent smile which she was known for. Her eyebrows rose, and a frown overtook her face as it succumbed to concern for his well-being. "Mr. William's, are you okay? Ray just nodded slowly as his eye's raced around; he knew something was wrong, but he just couldn't quite put his finger on it. At that moment, Ray jumped back to his feet, and he started to back away as his eyes widened.

"You ain't her. You can't be." Due to how far back he was in conjunction with how dark the room was, the only thing he could make out was the silhouette of Elaine. Ray looked in terror as it slowly rose to a sitting-up position and repositioned itself to where it looked as if it was now facing his general direction. Her head cocked over violently as if the muscles in the neck could no longer withstand the weight of her head and gravity just overtook it. Elaine's voice changed from that sweet innocent voice that Ray had come to love into one that sounded raspy and high pitched. "What are you talking about, Mr. Williams? Of course it's me, don't you remember all of those fond memories we had?"

Elaine pulled her body out of bed; her silhouette looked like a puppet being pulled up by the strings. Her head never changed position as she slowly staggered across the floor toward him. Ray continued moving backward until his back was against the cold wall. Elaine progressed slowly until she eventually reached a spot where the moonlight illuminated her face. To Ray's terror, the once beautiful face he came to love was now wholly morphed into an empty shell of what she once was.

Her hair still maintained the same blond color that it had prior, but it was now full of dirt and knots. Part of her hair that wasn't all clumped up covered her right eye, concealing what was left behind it, while the left was completely bare. This, in conjunction with the way moonlight was hitting Elaine, showed an empty eye socket that had previously housed her light blue eyes. Her fair skin lost the youthful warm glow that it had prior and was replaced with a grayish, almost green color. Any part of her flesh could be seen, looked as if it were completely devoid of muscle, leaving behind a skeleton covered in decaying skin. Elaine's full, lush lips had almost completely disappeared, now displaying significantly decomposed gums barely holding the teeth in place.

"Stay the hell away from me!" Ray yelled as she was now only a few feet away and continuing to decrease the distance between them. Elaine disregarded his command, making it just farther than kissing distance, and placed her cold boney hand around his throat. She brought her head in next to his ear and whispered in that shrill voice. "I have something important to tell you, Mr. Williams." Ray's face was turning red as he struggled to breathe, and he was using his hands to try and pry Elaine's hand off of around his throat.

Elaine slowly pulled her head away from his ear and stared toward him with her hollow eye sockets. His frantic grip on her hand became loose as his hands slowly fell to the wayside as he became blue from the lack of oxygen. "You're not long for the living." Elaine then let go of her grip as Ray's body hit the floor while saying, "yet you're not long for the world of the dead either." His skin slowly changed from the blue color that it had obtained into a paler version of his normal skin tone, and he leaned over, vomiting a large amount of blood. Elaine's jaw dropped as if surprised by what was happening.

Placing both hands to the floor in an attempt to stabilize himself, Ray started to laugh in between, taking deep breaths. The chuckles started out relatively tame, but as the frequency increased, the malice in each laugh did as well. Ray forced himself to his knees, his eyes glowing a dark red color, almost a blood-red, as he looked up at Elaine. "You are not her. You can't be. She is dead and has been dead for years now." He then got up to his feet and started walking slowly toward Elaine. "So tell me, what are you? Why do you torture me so?" His beloved then started to back away, "What are you talking about, Mr. Williams? It's me, your love Elaine."

Ray just shook his head while his face was displaying a snarl at this point. "No, it's not; you are a fake!" Elaine started backing up at this point. Each step that she took caused her to regain her youthful glow. "Mr. Williams, you are scaring me!" she said, now looking once again as the Elaine that he remembered. A malicious smile came to his face, increasing the fear that she felt, which the laugh from earlier caused. "As you should be. I know I would be scared too if I were in your shoes." Ray's voice almost had a growl in it, as Elaine eventually backed up to the point where she hit the edge of the bed. Unable to continue stepping backward any further, she fell to her butt and hands as she attempted to crawl backward away from Ray. Meanwhile, he continued making strides across the floor until he met her at the bed where she lay prior.

Tears poured down her face while she was shaking violently, whether or not this was really Elaine, this being showed every sign of true terror. "Please, Mr. Williams, you don't have to do this!" Ray's upper lip began to quiver, and his mouth began to drool excessively like a rabid dog. "Stop!" Ray yelled, "I think we both know this was long overdue." Ray then used his left hand to jerk Elaine's head toward the upper left, thus exposing her neck. Ray's breathing became heavier, and all he felt was sharp pain pierce the gums just in front of his canine teeth and became unbearably thirsty. Once the pain stopped, he thrust his mouth toward Elaine's neck, sinking his teeth into it. She was able to get anything more than a squeak out before she succumbed to the bite, much like a mouse falling victim to the bite of a rattlesnake. Her warm blood filled Ray's mouth much like cold beers had prior, and after a few moments, her tensed-up body became limp.

After drinking as much blood as possible, he pulled himself back from the corpse. His face was shocked by what he saw lying in front of him. Where Elaine was prior laid a creature that he had never seen. Its eyes were wide open and pitch black. Instead of a human's nose, two nasal cavities were indented in the skin on the area where it would have been. Elaine's mouth became a long proboscis with sharp fangs at its end, circling around the inner part of the opening. Her skin transformed into a greyish color again as her soft hands transformed into sharp claws. Ray took a few deep breaths to make sense of everything, and after what felt like a few seconds, his head shot up from where he was sleeping.

At this point, Ray was sweating and hyperventilating, trying to calm himself down as he started looking around for the other two men. They were sleeping, each at different spots around the fire that was starting to dim out. He chuckled to himself. "So much for keeping watch." Ray then pulled himself up off the ground and stepped a little closer to the fire. Using what was left of it to get a little light, he rummaged around in his satchel until he grabbed the pocket watch and took it out. "I wonder what time it is?" He opened the lid and tilted the watch at an angle to get a good read of the minute and second hands. Squinting at it, he could make out the watch displaying four o'clock. Ray then looked over toward the eastern sky to confirm if the watch was working correctly. Way on yonder, on the horizon, Ray noticed that the sky had a purple tint to it. This not only showed that the watch was still in working order but also that it wasn't that far off, if at all. If Ray's education guess was accurate, they had maybe an hour or two max before the sun rose. He then turned himself toward the north and held his pocket watch in his hand again, gripping the sides and saying, "I want to find Travis Anthony Fowler." Much like last time, the second handspun quickly around and stopped at the sixty-second mark. Ray smiled as he knew that if they had moved any farther, It was at least in the same direction that they were headed.

Without a moment's notice, the wind picked up a strong gust taking fire out and robbing Ray of what little light he had. He quickly slipped the watch back into his satchel, and another stronger gust of wind shot into Ray, knocking him on his ass. Never experiencing winds that felt so strong or targeted, Ray looked around frantically for anything that could have caused what was happening. After a few seconds, his eyes were finally adjusting to the dark.

Still, before Ray could get a good look, another powerful gust of wind came slamming into his chest, causing him to fall to his back and gasp for air. Looking up toward the sky, Ray vaguely saw a figure that looked like a cowboy on a horse through the darkness. The interesting thing about the horse was that the bottom half of its body morphed into what looked like a dark cloud. The wind finally let up, giving Ray a chance to breathe and draw both of his birds of prey revolvers. The creature turned toward Ray and dashed forward with such speed that it was almost instantly in his face. Its eyes were pale white circles surrounded by two large dark hollow sockets. The skin on both the human-like and horse-like creature matched being as pale as possible. Both the horse-like creature's mane and the human-like creature's hair matched in length along with the shade of black. The creature's mouth opened wider than a snake does, with its jaw unhinged as it let out an ear-piercing shriek. This caused Ray to yell out in pain as he fired multiple shots at the creatures. The creature's face turned into a menacing smile as it moved back into a position high in the sky.

Ray? Are you okay?" Mavrick asked as he ran over to help, placing a hand out for him in an attempt to pull him off the ground. "Do I look okay to you?" he asked as he slipped the Birds of Prey back into their holsters and then drew the pistol that he retrieved from the soul hunter. After Mavrick pulled Ray up, he asked him, "What happened?" Before Ray could mutter even a syllable, a giant gust of wind caught him off guard again, throwing him to the ground. This time the pressure from the wind kept pressing on his chest, making it so that he couldn't breathe. Ray then pointed up in the sky toward the creature, mouthing help.

Unfortunately, due to the consistent pressure placed on him, he couldn't actually get out any sound. Making matters worse, with it still being dark, both Gabriel and Mavrick had a hard time understanding what he was trying to communicate with them. The creature all of a sudden shot back down to where everyone was, displaying its terrifying shriek, almost as if trying to warn the two other men to stay back. Not one to take orders from most, Mavrick took out his knife and attempted to swing at the creature. This didn't affect the creature even a little bit as the blade just phased through it.

Gabriel then suggested that Mavrick try to hit it with his revolver. Mavrick looked back, shocked, almost as if he were offended by the idea. "What? You got to be kidding me." Gabriel insisted, "Seriously, try it!" Mavrick shook his head and mumbled under his breath to himself, "This is stupid. If the knife didn't work, why the hell would a revolver?" as he slid the knife back into its sheave, and he drew his revolver. Mavrick then pistol-whipped the creature across the humanoid's face. The creature let out a loud shriek as it vanished, and the wind completely let off of Ray.

For a few moment's Ray lay there coughing and gasping for air for a few moments while Mavrick questioned Gabriel, "How the hell did you know that was going to work?" His voice contained a mixture of astonishment and disbelief. Gabriel shrugged and said, "Honestly, I didn't, but my grandfather was always extremely superstitious. And I remembered him telling me when I was a kid that if I ever needed to fend off evil spirits to use iron." Mavrick re-holstered his weapon as he bent over, reaching out his hand to re-assist Ray up off the ground. Once on his feet again, Ray took a few more deep breaths in an attempt to regain his composure. Finally regaining some of his strength, he instructed Gabriel to grab the horses and asked Mavrick to pick up any of their equipment that may be lying around. The wind started to pick up heavily again, and Ray started yelling, "Be quick now; I got a feeling we just pissed it off!"

Thankfully for Mavrick, there wasn't that much equipment laying out. It was a few things that Gabriel and Mavrick placed out to make their camp a little more comfortable while Ray was sleeping, so it took him about a minute to round up everything. Once he had all the equipment stacked up in his arms and made his way back to where Ray was standing, Gabriel was back with the horses. Mavrick then took the pile of equipment over to his horse, placed it on the back of its saddle, and began to tie it down. Meanwhile, Gabriel pulled himself upon his horse as Ray made his way onto Old Red.

Now with the items secured, Mavrick proceeded to pull himself up onto the side of his when suddenly the wind rustled up violently again. This time a massive gust of wind shot out of the sky and slammed into Gabriel, causing him to fly backward off his horse. With the way it hit him, he ended up doing a backflip and then hitting the ground face first, causing a massive splatter of mud to shoot up around him. The creature then swooped down, forcing a constant flow of wind against the back of his head. Gabriel was trying to hold his breath as much as he could as he was pushing with all of his might against the ground in an attempt to get free, but it was no use. "Hang on, Gabriel; I gotcha!" Ray yelled as he aimed the Soul hunter's pistol that he still had drawn. After letting out a deep breath, he pulled the trigger, and a blue flame hotter than hellfire shot through the air making contact with the odd creature. The air pressure let up off Gabriel as the creature looked straight up to the air and let out a shriek which caused all three men to yell out in pain as they covered their ears in a feeble attempt to muffle the sound.

    The creature started flailing around violently as the wound ended up becoming lit by the blue fire. Quickly it traveled to the rest of its body, eventually completely consuming it. This led to the creature and the flame disappearing into a cloud of smoke, leaving nothing more behind than the smell of sulfur. Ray slid the soul hunter's pistol back into his duster's inner chest pocket while Mavrick hopped off his horse for a moment pulling Gabriel up off the ground. Ray loosened his grip on the pistol, and as he removed his hand from inside of his duster, he asked Gabriel, "Are you okay?". Standing at this point, Gabriel's face was pale as a ghost, and his eyes were as wide as could be. After a moment of processing what just happened, he quietly answered Ray in a monotone voice, "Yeah, I believe that I am. What the hell was that?". Ray responded, "Based on how it looked, my guess it was a spirit wrangler." Gabriel looked completely caught off guard by this response. "Are you sure? What even is it?" Ray rubbed his hand through his facial hair as he thought through his answer. Back where I'm from, when you're a kid, that creature is a boogeyman of sorts. Parents used to tell their kids about them and how they would abduct them if they didn't listen. Stories said that if it takes a person with evil in their heart, and one of those things kills them, they become cursed to ride in the skies for all eternity. "

Gabriel was slightly shaking a bit, clearly from his encounter. "Well, I'm happy that didn't happen, but Ray, what did you use to get rid of it? Nothing Mavrick or I seemed to affect it." Ray just chuckled while acting as if it was a small feat. "I have a pistol to thank for that. I picked it up on my travels." Gabriel just stared at Ray with a blank stare as he continued responding in his enthusiastic tone. " I see." Gabriel and Mavrick then pulled themselves back onto their respective horses. Ray turned Old Red around, causing him to face the two other men. He proceeded to look them up and down, analyzing them in an attempt to ensure that they were ready. "I just wanted to say that I appreciate both of you for everything that y'all have done. I don't know what to expect going forward, but we can overcome it as long as we stick together. Are y'all ready to ride?" Both Gabriel and Mavrick glanced at each other then looked back at Ray. Both of them acknowledged him by nodding their heads slightly. Ray nodded back toward both of them out of respect as he turned Old Red back toward the north and proceeded to guide them to their next destination.

Chapter 15 Ghost Town Showdown

After spending most of the day heading north on the horses, the three men came across an old town around dusk. From a quick glance, the town looked completely empty. Due to them riding for so long without stopping, and this seemed to be the only place within miles, they decided to take a moment to rest. Gabriel started riding in toward the center of town, but before he made it even an inch ahead of Ray, he stopped him "Wait, before you head in, look." Ray started rummaging around through this satchel, pulling out the pocket watch again, securely grasping it in the palm of his hand. The watch pointed directly toward the center of town. "I'm not certain, but I have a feeling that these bastards are near." Ray looked over the watch carefully, noticing that the second hand seemed to be moving around in quick, small jerks. Unlike before, where it was far more steady. Before we go any farther, we should devise a plan so that we ain't putting ourselves into a bad spot."

Mavrick and Gabriel nodded, acknowledging what Ray was saying. Mavrick then pitched his idea "I think what we should do is head in from different angles. Ray can head in through the main road, while Gabriel goes in from behind the buildings on the west side of town, and I would head in from the east side. Ray, once you get a good look in town, Gabriel and I will wait until we hear you yell all clear. Once you give the signal, we will meet up with you in the middle of town." Gabriel nodded slightly "Not a bad idea Mavrick; I'm okay with that if you are Ray."

Ray sighed slightly from exhaustion, "I like the idea, but before we go through with it, there is one last thing we need to do." Both men looked at each other, their eyes were wide, and their faces had a puzzled look on them. They then simultaneously looked back at Ray as he unmounted his horse and began pulling something of decent size off of the side of the horse. Once it was free from the horse, the men could see a gun. Ray walked over to Gabriel and tossed it up to him. Snatching it out of the air, he asked, "Why are you handing me a gun?" Ray responded, "This my friend, is going to be the firepower that you need. I'm lending you my silver wolf shotgun." Ray's serious demeanor loosened up a bit as a slight smirk came across his face. "Remember, I said lending, I want it back when we make it out alive." Gabriel nodded as he pulled his hat down to the point that concealed his eyes as he rode off to his vantage point.

Before Mavrick had a chance to take off, Ray stopped him "If we find the Shopkeeper's daughter alive and I don't make it through this, promise me that you will get her home safe." Mavrick nodded slightly and then rode to the location where he would await the signal. Ray made his way back over to Old Red and remounted him. The two of them then trotted down the main road towards the center of town. Ray started coughing violently when they made it about halfway down the road. Small gasps of air could be heard between them as he attempted to regain control of his breathing. After a few moments of uncontrolled coughing, he could finally breathe again.

Ray then used what little strength he had to wipe the accumulation of blood off of his mouth with the side of his closed fist. At this point, he noticed that his breathing was also getting heavier, and the world felt like it was spinning. This felt similar to his experience of being drunk but on a much more intense scale. Ray began sweating profusely. "I just have to keep focused on finding that bastard; I will make it through this." One of the first buildings Ray came across as he entered town had a hitch in front of it. He then positioned Old Red to make hitching him up as easy as possible, ensuring that he was secured. Ray also confirmed that he wasn't in a position where his guard would be down for long. He then patted his horse's side, comforting him, "Don't worry, buddy, everything's going to be okay." Ray double-checked his satchel to ensure he had everything he needed and reloaded the Birds of Prey revolvers. Once as prepared as could be, he took a deep breath and followed the muddy road into the heart of the town.

It could have been due to the time of night it was or the gravity of the situation. Whatever the reason, the town produced a very eerie feeling. The only light that Ray had to go by was the moon and what looked like a small lantern that lit way in the center of town. The buildings seemed to be run down. Long weeds and small trees seemed to be wedging their way out of the floorboards of porches. As he was walking past them, Ray noticed that the lack of light made it impossible to see anything on the interior of the buildings. However, based on the porch's condition, he could make an educated guess of how the interior of the building was. Ray placed his right on his right revolver as he slowly came into reaching distance of the lantern's position. Not only did it assist in illuminating the area a bit, but in some ways, it assisted in making the atmosphere even more creepy. Ray had a horrible feeling about this place at this point. Not only was it being lit a strong indication that someone was near or possibly still here, but they were also entirely surrounded by woods. It was almost as if the trees themselves were taunting him, reaching for him as if they wanted to consume him.

As Ray made his way around the center of the town, he looked for any movement that signified a trap or someone expecting company. No such signs were being present; he took as deep of a breath as his body would allow and started yelling to draw him out if he was there. "Travis Fowler, come out here now, you dumb son of a bitch!" Within what felt like seconds, all of the buildings, which looked empty prior, had a bunch of men start flooding out of them. These men wore black leather dusters and hats to match. Suddenly out of the top floor of an old worn-down bar, which was located in the right corner of town, a dark figure emerged, stepping between two men. This one was different because he walked with pride and being closer to the other two men almost made it look like he was being guarded. The figure proceeded to laugh, revealing two fangs. Ray could only make them out thanks to the dim light from the lantern.

The figure began antagonizing him; his voice sounded rough, almost like having a bit of a growl behind it. "Boy, you sure are a bright one, ain't you. Tell me, why in the world would you think it was a good idea to go into a Rattler's den?" Ray's serious look stayed plastered across his face, his eyes locked onto the figure. "I think you know why I'm here, you sorry son of a bitch. Now, why don't you answer my question? Where is the girl?" The man started laughing as he alternated looking between the other two men on each side of him. "The girl? You're going to have to be a little bit more specific with that friend." Ray started to scowl; if looks could kill at this point, his eyes would be daggers. "You know which girl, the one from that damn mineshaft when you did this to me!"

The figure's laugh ceased, turning into a massive grin once again displaying its two fangs. "I don't think you know what you're talking about. Regardless, it doesn't matter. This is the second time you trespassed in our terrain; because of that, you're lucky to even be standing right now." Ray looked around, trying to ensure that no one was about to make a move, and then his eyes locked back onto the figure again. At this point, Ray's voice shook violently as he yelled at the figure with all of his rage. "Why would you do this to me?!" Before he could get another syllable out, another violent coughing fit took over. At the same time, he thought to himself, *not this, not now.* The figure waited for Ray to stop coughing before continuing.

"Well, that is simple, you see, you killed off a majority of my men, and honestly, I didn't like that. So after that little incident, I figured I would enjoy myself with a little treat and then give you my gift. Either way, I saw it; it was a win-win. Scenario one, you die from this more advanced form of tuberculosis, and then I have one less asshole to deal with. Scenario two, this advanced form of tuberculosis kills you. Once deceased, you would reanimate into a shadow of your former self. The plus side to this scenario is that you share my blood, which would allow me to influence you in your decisions. In turn, you would become the newest addition to my band of outlaws. Oh, and not to scare you, but most of the people I have given this gift to in the past have passed on." The figure started laughing as Ray fought to get his breathing under control.

Meanwhile, Ray looked around vigorously for any form of shelter that he could get to quickly when the bullets started flying. Unfortunately, there wasn't anything close, so if he had any chance of making it out of the bullet storm that was brewing, he would have to be quick. The figure's laugh transformed into a smirk again as the figure asked Ray, "So, is there anything else, or are you ready to die?" Ray's glare remained intensely focused on the figure as he stood at the ready, only having two shots he knew he had to make them count. If he missed, that was it. Swiftly Ray drew his Birds of Prey revolvers, taking out the two men surrounding the dark figure. Still, before he had a chance to move, a barrage of bullets was shot from all directions surrounding him. Ray yelled out in pain as the bullets pierced through with the ease of a knife in butter. Blood spewed out of his mouth and all of the holes that now filled his body. Ray's limp body fell hard to his knees, and he ended up falling forward into the mud. This caused it to splatter, shooting out in every direction.

Both Gabriel and Mavrick took cover, utilizing the edge of a building on their side of town as they entered the town's center from their respective position. Looking in shock, they saw Ray's body lying there, face down in a combination of his blood and the mud which the road was composed of. Mavrick was so pissed that he began yelling at the outlaws. "You sons of bitches, he was a good man! Y'all are going to die for this!" Mavrick had his Peacemakers at the ready and started open firing as he began open firing starting with the balcony of what looked like an old bank.

Taking two shots with the revolver in his left hand, he hit one of the men in the chest, incapacitating him and the other in the head, killing him immediately. Mavrick then fired two shots at the men at the top of the general store with his left one, taking out both of them as well. This was when three men sprinted out onto the porch from within the bar to get a better shot. However, before any of them could get a shot off, Gabriel ran forward until he was at a reasonable distance. He then shot the Silver Wolf shotgun, filling the three men with bullets. Two men then made their way out of the Bar's swinging doors and started to open fire on Gabriel. Thankfully the only shot that got off missed before Mavrick's revolvers filled the two of them full of lead.

To Mavrick's surprise, there was a loud splat in the mud behind him. Looking back, it was one of the outlaws, and it almost landed on top of him. Mavrick thought that the person was potentially trying to shoot him over the ledge and just lost his balance. Still, after examining the body, he quickly discovered multiple bullet wounds. Looking back toward Gabriel's position, he saw that he was back in his position behind the building and was holding a pistol that had smoke rising from the barrel. The mud right next to Mavrick started splattering like crazy as four guys from the bar began open firing on him. This, in turn, caused him to throw himself back into cover against the wall to get into cover. Mavrick leaned over just enough to get a peak in an attempt to estimate where he was going to need to shoot. Still, before he could even get a glance, the bullets whizzed past him, forcing him to get back into cover. "Damn it!" Mavrick mumbled to himself as he tried to figure out the easiest way to stop the storm of bullets that were raining down upon him.

     Gabriel then stepped out, taking a shot toward one of the buildings on the same side of the town that Mavrick was on. He could only get a few shots off with his pistol before he had to quickly run back behind cover. A ton of bullets shot up the side of the building, causing its residue to turn into a cloud of dust to build up beside him. Thanks to him taking the focus off Mavrick for a moment, he peeked back around the edge for a moment and whispered to himself. "Now, I just have to find a way to get an idea of how many more of these guys there are." Before he was able to attempt to do anything, a few more bullets whizzed past his head, forcing him back behind cover. Mavrick yelled toward Gabriel in hopes that he could hear his request over the tinnitus due to the gunfire. "Gabriel, we need to figure out how many of them there are; try to take a look, and I will cover you!" Gabriel nodded hesitantly as he slowly attempted to peek around the corner to see what he could see. Unfortunately, he couldn't even look around the corner before getting shot at. Seeing this, Mavrick knew that the men had them like sitting ducks at this point. Even slightly, if they went into the open, they would be as good as dead.

"Gabriel! When I say go, I need you to open fire on them, okay!?" Mavrick instructed him. Gabriel was scowling, clearly irritated with the suggestion. "Are you trying to get us killed!?" Mavrick answered with a slight growl, slightly irritated with the pushback. "Gabriel, I need you to trust me. If you don't, we are going to die!" Gabriel shook his head as he let out a loud sigh. "Fine!" Mavrick was standing with his back against the wall as his arms crossed across his chest, still holding both revolvers tightly. "NOW!" he shouted as Gabriel ran out from cover and started open firing on the outlaws, and they returned them tenfold. While that was going on, Mavrick ended up slipping his left revolver into his holster and sliding off his duster. He then took it in his left hand and sort of whipped out around the corner and let go. The men started opening fire on it, while Mavrick utilized this as the slight advantage he needed, allowing him to slide out from behind cover. After redrawing his left revolver and bringing both handguns to the ready, he joined Gabriel in firing back.

The first two shots Gabriel took ended up taking out two men on the second-floor balcony of what looked like an old inn. Their heads whipped back violently as the bullets made contact with each of their skulls. This produced a loud crack followed by two thuds as their bodies ended up hitting the ground. Mavrick quickly skimmed over the area to figure out how many more of them there were. From what he could see, there were around ten of them in his line of sight. Six of them were located on the balconies, while the other four were scattered across a few of the porches. As he finished taking mental notes, the outlaws continued firing at Mavrick. While he had been lucky for the most part, one of the bullets almost got him in the chest. Thankfully he slid out of the way as the bullet traveled through where he was standing prior, and then he rolled back up into a standing position. He continued running until he had complete control of his balance again and shot off two rounds. These shots were aimed at two more of the outlaws located up in one of the balconies. The first shot was an instakill as it hit the first man in the head, leaving behind a trail of bone fragments and blood. The second shot was also effective at incapacitating the second outlaw. He collapsed forward while the bullet penetrated his chest. This no doubt hit some of the vital organs, which in turn led to him screaming in pain as his body flung forward violently as he collapsed to the wooden floorboards in pain.

Thanks to Mavrick's move, most outlaws shifted their attention to him. This gave Gabriel a chance to really aim and attempt to cause as much damage as possible. Making one of the guys that were closer to him on a porch his target, he closed one eye, took aim, and ended up piercing the outlaw's head with one shot. His head jerked back, and his body followed to fall back until it was stopped by the outside wall of the old building, letting out a loud thud. A few more shots came Mavrick's way, and he slid out of the way, dodging them like had the bullets prior. This time he ended up taking two shots with his revolvers mid-slide, this time taking out two men on the ground floor of the old bank. The guy on the left went down quickly with a headshot, but the one on the right ended up just taking a bullet in his left leg. The only reason Mavrick was able to tell this was because when he was shot, the man collapsed forward and fell straight down to the floor. On top of that, rather than being instantly unconscious, he could be heard screaming in agonizing pain.

Gabriel took aim with his pistol at one of the men on top of the general store. He then took his shot, completely missing. The bullet flying past his ear caught the outlaw's attention. He then fired back at Gabriel out of retaliation, hitting his arm. This caused Gabriel to fall backward, his back hitting the ground while screaming in pain. Mavrick yelled out, "Gabriel, you okay!?" as he took a shot at two more of the men on one of the balconies. The bullets whizzed through the air making contact with the two men's skulls almost simultaneously. Inevitably both of their heads whipped back violently as the bodies dropped to the ground. All four of the remaining men shot at Mavrick. The first one missed hitting the mud next to him, causing it to splatter and him to stumble backward. This, in turn, caused the second, third and fourth bullets to whizz right past where he had previously been, essentially saving his life. Gabriel yelled out as he slowly struggled to crawl back behind cover. "Not really, the son of a bitch got me!" Mavrick pulled back the hammers of the revolvers as he yelled back in response. "Hang tight, Gabriel!"

    Mavrick raised one of the guns toward the direction of one of the buildings that was so weathered he couldn't make out what it used to be. The other revolver was facing the balcony of what looked to be the old jail. He pulled the triggers simultaneously, with both handguns sitting at different angles and directions. Both bullets raced out. The man on the old building ended up getting clipped first, hitting him in the chest and causing him to stumble backward. He then hit the wall of the building and slid down. Slowly The man's head tilted over as blood poured out of his mouth. The outlaw on the old jail's balcony head whipped back violently, and a thud could be heard as he hit the wooden floor of where he was standing. Mavrick then turned to the left and started running toward Gabriel. However, before he could reach him, one of the remaining outlaws from one of the building's balconies behind him took a shot with his pistol. The bullet hit him in the back of his left shoulder blade, which caused him to fall forward to his knees. "Shit!" He yelled as he looked back, placing his right revolver between his arm and his side. He then pointed the handgun behind himself, aiming at his assailant, and pulled the trigger. In an instant, the man fell backward much like many of the others prior.

Mavrick slowly pulled himself up off the muddy ground and continued toward his injured friend. As he did, without looking from Gabriel or even slowing down, he raised his revolver with his right hand. He finished off the last outlaw on the balcony with a gunshot to the head. He then made his way over to Gabriel's location, sliding both revolvers back into their holsters. Mavrick then extended out his right-hand, offering assistance with pulling him up off the ground. Mavrick's face squinted, and he grunted in pain as he instructed Gabriel, "Keep pressure on the wound." Gabriel nodded his head. His face was also squinting like Mavrick's from the pain. "I will. any idea where their leader went?" Mavrick shook his head. "No, but I feel like if he would've gone anywhere, it would have been back into the bar." Now that Gabriel was standing again, he ended scrunching up his sleeve tight enough to apply the pressure necessary to stop the bleeding.

Meanwhile, Mavrick drew his knife and cut his left shirt sleeve up near his shoulder. He then placed the sleeve on his wound and turned around, requesting that Gabriel would tie it for him. After securing it, Gabriel reloaded his pistols and Ray's shotgun, while Mavrick did the same with his Revolvers. Once they were as prepared as possible, both men made their way to opposite sides of the swinging doors, which were the entrance of the old saloon. Mavrick secured his back against the wall on the left side while Gabriel Mirrored him on the right.

With both men in position, Mavrick glanced over to Gabriel, nodding slightly. It was his non-verbal way of asking if he was ready. Gabriel nodded back after a moment of hesitation, looking Mavrick dead straight in his eyes. Mavrick saw the uncertainty, but both men knew that they were at a point of no return. Mavrick then whispered his plan to him. "Okay, Gabriel, we are going to bust in on the count of three. Wait for my cue." Sliding his left revolver into its holster, he placed his left hand in the air, holding up his first finger. Within seconds he added his middle finger and then his ring finger. Mavrick then threw his hand down, drew his left revolver again, and whispered "Now." in kind of a loud voice. Both men simultaneously burst through the swinging doors. Mavrick holding his firearms, and Gabriel holding Ray's shotgun. Two men popped up from behind one of the flipped tables and aimed at them. Still, before they had a chance to really do anything, Gabriel pulled the trigger on the shotgun, blowing them away.

    The inside of the bar was decaying almost as bad as the outside. Due to all of the wooden planks that made up the floor being filled with so many holes, both Mavrick and Gabriel were hesitant to go further due to fear of falling through it. A man suddenly popped out from behind the bar shooting at them; both men were able to dodge as the bullet whizzed right past them. Gabriel ended up ducking down toward the left, while Mavrick did the same toward the right, firing off two shots on his way down. The bullet from his right revolver missed the man completely, hitting an old mason jar filled with some weird liquid causing it to explode into a giant glass mess. However, the left bullet made direct contact with the man's skull, violently jerking it backward, forcing his body to follow as he collapsed to the floor. Mavrick tread slowly forward into the middle of the bar. Every step he took sounded like it amplified the sound of the creaking floorboards. This made him feel even more nervous as he thought it would assist the outlaws in catching them off guard. His eyes raced around in an attempt to pick up on any movement before anyone could catch them by surprise.

Suddenly, Gabriel could be heard yelling for a split second and then nothing. The sound of his voice was replaced by the sound of the swinging doors slowly swaying back and forth quickly. Mavrick turned around to see what was going on, and he started to perspire profusely. Where Gabriel had been standing prior was now empty, so without any hesitation, Mavrick rushed back through the swinging doors in an attempt to find him.

Once back outside, Mavrick saw Gabriel being held in the air by his throat by a figure in a long black trench coat wearing a black cowboy hat. Mavrick cocked back the hammer on each revolver and aimed them at him as he yelled, "Put him down, you stupid son of a bitch!" The figure then let out a deep laugh, his face turned slightly so that he could see Mavrick out of the corner of his eye, and then asked, "Give me one reason I should?" When Mavrick attempted to answer, nothing seemed to come out. He appeared to be choking on his words for a moment due to how intimidated he was. How couldn't he be? He had never fought anything that had the strength to pick up a man with one hand along with speed to move that quick. It had to be otherworldly, and Mavrick knew that the odds were already stacked against them. What could he do? After a second of hesitation, Mavrick took a deep breath and responded the only way that he knew how "I'll give you two." He then pulled the triggers of each revolver. The bullets passed through the area where the figure stood and completely unphased him.

Gabriel and the figure vanished into a black mist, suddenly appearing next to him about six feet over to the right. The figure then let out a deep, menacing laugh and told Mavrick, "I wouldn't have done that if I were you, you're just giving me more incentive to kill this one." Gabriel's face was turning red at this point, his hands on the man's grip in an attempt to get it to loosen. It was like watching a mouse trying to escape a snake's grip. Terror could be seen in Gabriel's eyes, and he tried everything to get loose but with no prevail. Mavrick started yelling at him again, pushing through the fear, "I'm warning you, let him go!" The figure turned his body around completely while still keeping a firm grip on Gabriel's neck, the smirk that it had prior vanished. This was the first time Mavrick could get a good look at him. The figure's face was as pale as a full moon. His eyes glowed a dark red color, and he had a massive beard made of coarse black hair up until right around his mouth. The hair around that area was black, but it seemed to be stained by something red. It almost looked as if he drank a ton of red wine and just never bothered to wash it out of his beard. In general, the man seemed to be pretty tall; he was at least a foot or two taller than Mavrick.

"And what exactly do you plan to do if I don't let him go? Mavrick hesitated for a moment due to being intimidated and then answered, "If you touch a hair on his head, I will shoot you dead. You hear me? Let him go!" The figure's face grew another malicious smile as he said, "If you insist." The words were cold, clearly full of ill intent as he looked Gabriel dead in the eye. "Remember, your friend asked for this." Gabriel's eyes widened as the fear struck him from the unknown he was about to endure. The man's hand then violently jerked to the side. Gabriel's neck let out a loud snapping sound, and then his body became limp. With no fight left in his body, the figure then tossed Gabriel to the side as if it were a rag doll.

Mavrick's face turned red as he started open firing with his revolvers on the figure, "You're going to pay for that, you twisted son of a bitch!". Mavrick was yelling so loud it could have woken the dead as he was alternating shots between both revolvers. Each bullet contacted the figure as he continued shooting in rapid succession. The crazy thing was that not even one bullet seemed to slow him down as he nonchalantly continued to walk over to where Mavrick was standing.

It was almost as if he was shooting a ghost as the only thing that seemed to seep from his body was a smoke-like substance. This smoke only seemed to show up in the areas where he was shot, and it didn't seem to last much longer than a few seconds, after which the smoke seemed to vanish completely. The shots didn't even leave even a scar behind to indicate any damage. At this point, the figure was but a mere few steps away from Mavrick. In response, he raised his Revolvers toward the figure's head. "Die, you bastard!" He yelled, pulling the triggers rapidly. The Figure's head looked almost as if it were vibrating as he continued, walking toward Mavrick, his malicious smirk never leaving his face. The sound of the bullets firing out of the guns was quickly replaced by clicking as the revolver started dry firing. The figure is now just outside of arm's reach from Mavrick.

The figure's smirk quickly evolved into an evil smile, baring his fangs and all, "You done?" Mavrick was drenched in sweat at this point; his eyes widened, displaying the fear that he was truly feeling. Mavrick then slid his pistols back into his holster and unsheathed his knife. In a feeble attempt, he tried to swing at the outlaw. Before he could make contact, the man had a firm grip on Mavrick's hand, and he twisted it violently, causing it to make a cracking sound as he dropped the knife and screamed out in pain. The figure's smirk increased in size as he taunted him, "Boy, you are just asking to die, ain't you."

With ungodly speed the figure cocked his fist back, and he then shot it forward across Mavrick's jaw, using his drawback for as much power as possible. This caused his head to shoot to the side. As he attempted to bring it back to his usual position, the figure already had a fully loaded punch headed straight for his face again. This time, the outlaw's fist made contact with Mavrick's right eye; this let out a loud crack which could be heard quietly behind a loud pain-filled grunt. Before he had a chance to respond, the figure drove his knee into Mavrick's abdominal area. This caused his head to jerk forward violently as Mavrick began aggressively gasping for air. The figure cocked his fist back again, this time from an underhand position. He then used his leverage and unnatural strength to uppercut Mavrick. He put all of his force in this punch, causing Mavrick to come off the ground for a moment, fly backward and land on his back.

The figure then slowly walked over to where Mavrick laid, looking as if he wasn't even winded from their confrontation. Mavrick, on the other hand, was rolling around in pain and continued to struggle with even catching his breath. That ill intent-filled smile returned to the outlaw's face. "See now, I tried to warn you, there is nothing you can do to me." Mavrick started coughing up blood while the world around him began to spin rapidly. The outlaw then snatched Mavrick up by the throat, slowly lifting him above his head. "You got any final requests?" Mavrick's face was turning red at this point as he kept both of his hands firm on the figure's grip, unable to speak. The figure laughed menacingly, baring his fangs. "Guess not. In that case, it's time to die." The figure started to increase the pressure behind his grip. Mavrick's eyes widened briefly and quickly closed as his body became limp.

"Pathetic." the outlaw said to himself as he was about to toss him aside. As soon as he went to release his grip, Mavrick's right hand shot up, getting a solid grasp on his wrist. The eye that wasn't blindfolded suddenly opened up and stared at him with a feral look in it. He then cocked his left hand back and struck the figure right in the nose. The outlaw's grip loosened, dropping Mavrick and the power from the strike proved to be strong enough to get him to stumble back a few steps. Quickly he regained his footing before tripping backward and ending up in a pile of mud. The figure's smile vanished as he shook off the punch.

"That one actually hurt. What are you? Mavrick's only verbal responses were grunts and growls as he was hunched up, just sitting in the mud. His mouth and nose started to morph into more of a snout. The sound of cracking could be heard as his body transformed from its original form into something with a lot more mass and much more animalistic. Thanks to him growing at such a fast rate, his clothing began to tear and rip. The hair on his body thickened drastically and seemed to spread to every part of it. His ears shifted positions from the side of his head, up toward the top of it. Letting out a loud scream. Mavrick's voice quickly turned into a sharp howl.

The massive creature that was now standing where Mavrick was. It snarled its huge fangs toward the outlaw.

"Well, well, I had no idea that you had such a creature residing in you. Not that it matters, you're only delaying the inevitable." the figure said as he sprinted toward Mavrick. He was moving so fast that he seemingly vanished, only to reappear in front of the creature with his fist striking Mavrick in his stomach. This caused him to fall to his back. The figure dashed over to where Mavrick was lying and attempted to stomp his black boot down hard on his head. Mavrick swung full force with his claw, clipping his leg, in turn causing the outlaw to stumble backward. Looking down at his knee, the figure saw a massive scratch. He then let out a sigh as he looked back toward him. Now starting to get mad, his voice shook as he glared at Mavrick out of rage. "You're going to pay for that, you stupid dog!" Mavrick flipped himself back to all fours as he responded to the figure's comment by displaying his massive fangs and growling.

The figure started to sprint toward Mavrick quickly, but thanks to the damage he took, he was no longer running at speeds that made him invisible. The outlaw made it to where he was almost directly in front of him, and as he went to cock his fist back for another swing, Mavrick lunged forward, swinging his right front claw toward him. Both of their attempts proved to be to no avail as the figure was unable to make any contact before he had to pull back, and he was just a few inches away from the tip of Mavrick's claw.

The figure saw a slight opening as Mavrick tried to recuperate his composure from his swipe. Running up to him from the side, he hit him with a left hook, then a right, both on the side of his ribs. Each hit produced a sound similar to thunder crackling through the sky. Mavrick swung his right claw, digging his claws deep into the outlaw's face, causing it to jerk toward the left. The figure then slowly turned his head back, looking at Mavrick with a snarl on his face. He then punched Mavrick in the face and quickly shot his left hand to the back of Mavrick's neck while bringing his right hand to the front of Mavrick's throat. With all of his might, the outlaw picked Mavrick up off of the ground and slammed him into the mud, causing a massive impression in it. The figure then drew back his leg and kicked the wolf-like creature so hard across the face that it caused him to slide across the ground a few inches.

Mavrick started pushing himself up off the ground as the outlaw ran over, grabbing him by the back of the head, and proceeded to slam his head into the ground multiple times. Right when he went to slam it down the third time, Mavrick took his massive claw and grabbed ahold of the figure's leg. With a firm grip wrapped around it, Mavrick rolled over onto his back, causing the figure to quickly lose his balance. This made him fall backward and get flung through the air like a ragdoll as Mavrick released him. Due to the massive momentum of his roll in conjunction with his strength, a loud crack could be heard as the outlaw hit the wall of the old jail. That sound was then followed by loud thuds as he and the part of the wall he hit collapsed inside the building.

Mavrick fell to all four legs and sprinted over to the opening in the building that the figure had just made. He then pulled back his head back opened his massive jaws. His razor-sharp teeth were bared as he started to lunge toward the outlaw. Still, right as he was a few inches from sinking his teeth into him, the figure jerked his right hand up, securing a strong grip on Mavrick's throat. His eyes then shot open as he used his left hand to push himself up off the ground. Now standing, the outlaw slowly lifted his hand up as high as possible, bringing Mavrick up with it. Mavrick was biting toward him like a dog with rabies as his claws were flailing around wildly. Before the figure could do anything, one of Mavrick's claws ended up catching his stomach, digging deeply into it.

The outlaw was scowling at him at this point. "You're starting to really piss me off, you mangy mutt." He began punching Mavrick in the face, each punch releasing a loud crack as his knuckles made contact with him. Before the figure could get a fourth hit in, Mavrick's left claw shot up, swiping at the figure's fist knocking it out of the way. He then followed that up with his right claw swinging up, nicking the figure in the face. This, in turn, led to the figure dropping Mavrick, jerking around violently, and concealing his face as the tips of the claws grazed it. As he slowly turned his head back toward Mavrick, he ended up drawing a revolver that was in his holster and his knife in his other hand. He then yelled with a deep growl in his voice, "Die mutt!" as he started to open fire on Mavrick. Once the first bullet made contact with his left shoulder, Mavrick fell onto all fours, letting out a vicious roar, and burst into a full sprint. He was moving at speeds that made horses seem substantially slower. The second round from the revolver hit Mavrick hit his right arm, causing him to wail out in pain, but still not slowing him down. The third bullet that came out of the revolver shot right by Mavrick's head, almost hitting him. Before the figure could get another shot off, Mavrick slammed into him at full force, causing him to fall backward and slide through the mud once again. This time when he made contact with a wall, there wasn't enough pressure to penetrate it.

The outlaw began to aim again, but before he could take a shot, Mavrick caught up to him and sank his sharp teeth around the arm of the hand that held the revolver. The figure then flipped his knife around, holding it in a reversed, edge-out position. He then started to stab Mavrick in the back of the neck multiple times, causing him to bleed excessively as his growling just continued to get louder and deeper. When the outlaw impaled him the third time with the knife, Mavrick bit down as hard as he was able and then jerked his head away violently. This caused a loud cracking sound to come from the bone in his arm, along with a tearing sound from his skin and muscle being ripped apart from the rest of the body with relative ease. The immense pain shot through the outlaw's body as he ended up writing over in pain. Falling to the ground out of shock and pain, he dropped the knife, which caused it to drop into the mud. Within seconds Mavrick turned his head away from the amputated forearm, dropping it right next to the knife, and his fierce eyes locked on the outlaw. He was now on his back, using his remaining hand and legs to attempt to crawl away. Still, before he could make much progress, Mavrick dropped to all fours again and burst out into a full sprint.

Once Mavrick loomed over the outlaw, he pulled his head back, baring his razor-sharp teeth in preparation to sink them into the figure. The figure was able to get a grip on his knife. Mavrick made it a few inches away from his throat as the outlaw swung the knife toward Mavrick's face, thrusting it into his temple. This caused him to let out a violent howl as he fell over and the world went dark.

Once Mavrick opened his eyes, sat up, and looked around. It looked as if it were still late due to the moonlight shining down on the town. Looking around, he saw many bodies lying on the floorboards of the old porches from the shoot out along with a bunch of marks in the mud that indicated something massive being in the area, something inhuman. With further inspection of the mud, he noticed that it looked like it had blood mixed in with it. "What the hell happened?" he said to himself, scratching his head. The last thing that he remembered happening was being choked out by the leader of this gang. He then began wandering through the old town. He saw Gabriel's corpse lying in the mud. Tears started filling his eyes as his eyebrows rose. He then made his way over to him. "I'm so sorry, my friend." Mavrick said as he shook his head slowly, "No matter your past, I hope that you are redeemed in God's eyes."

Mavrick then remembered his promise to Ray. With this now in the forefront of his mind, he drew his revolvers, just in case he ran into any more trouble and searched all the buildings thoroughly. After what felt like an hour of thorough searching of the surrounding area, the shopkeeper's daughter was still nowhere to be found. As he let out an exhausted sigh, Mavrick slid the revolver back into his holster and decided that once he made it back to his horse, he was going to head back to Saint Edgerton. Mavrick figured that after everything that happened, he could use a drink. As he crossed back through the ghost town, he ended up passing where Ray was initially lying. Mavrick squinted and cocked his head sideways in confusion. Where Ray's corpse laid prior was now replaced with a muddy imprint of his body. "Weird." Mavrick said to himself, wondering about the outcome of Ray's body. With every step that Mavrick took toward his horse, his curiosity about his friend consumed him more and more. He began untying the reins from the old fence it had been secured to. Mavrick then made it to the horse's side and pulled himself up while he ran through many different questions, answering himself where he could. "What happened to Ray? Last I saw him, he was dead. Why would someone go through all the trouble of moving him? Why out here? Is there any real benefit to moving him? Where would they have moved him to? If it were near here, I would have spotted him when searching the buildings."

    Once secure on his horse, Mavrick kicked his heels into the side of it and made a clicking noise with his mouth. Once the horse picked up momentum, Mavrick pulled the reins firmly to the right causing the horse to turn left until he was completely facing the other direction. With the horse facing toward Saint Edgerton, Mavrick whipped the reins as he yelled "yeahhhhh!" as his horse took off like a bullet. As he rode, Mavrick's mind couldn't help but to race over everything, over and over, just being unable to shut it off. He consistently ran through the memory of both of his friends being killed in front of him, along with other things he just didn't quite understand. He couldn't help but wonder whether or not the shopkeeper's daughter was even still alive. If she was alive, how the hell was he even going to find her? As for the outlaw, he came toe to toe with whatever happened to him? Whatever the situation, there was no way he would rest with the possibility of something that evil just walking around. He needed to find him and make sure that he put an end to him once and for all. As for Ray, he knew his body vanishing didn't make sense. But if he was able to find that outlaw again, he would not only be able to get the answers he was looking for but also put an end to him for good this time. The only noise that could be heard the rest of the ride back was the sound of the horse galloping as the hoofs made contact with the ground. As for Mavrick, he continued to venture down the rabbit hole of thoughts and the possibilities.

Epilogue

Just like their trip to the ghost town, it took Mavrick almost an entire day to return to Saint Edgerton. Shook up and exhausted due to the traumatic experience that he had just endured, he figured he would head into the local saloon to wet his whistle. While doing so, he could sit down and start figuring out a game plan to track down the bastard that was responsible for his friend's demise. Finally, after what felt like an eternity, Mavrick made his way over to the Jack Eye's saloon. Even though the immense darkness, he could still see how poor the establishment's exterior was holding up.

Once Mavrick was a few feet away from the hitching post, he kicked his right foot over to the other side of his horse and slid down. His boots splattered a bit as they made contact with the mud. He then made his way to the front of the horse and led him until he was close enough to the post for the reins to reach. Mavrick then tied them to the hitching post and tugged them to ensure they were secured.

The old familiar creak could be heard as Mavrick started making his way up the decaying stairs, onto the porch, and through the doors, which looked like they were barely holding on. The inside of the saloon still looked like it did a few nights prior as if it was moments away from falling apart. Mavrick just continued past everything and walked up the bar, where he was greeted by the barkeep. This man was the same buff one with the handlebar mustache running the bar the other night.

"Hey friend, welcome back!" The barkeep greeted him while wiping down an empty glass. "What can I get for you?" Mavrick just leaned against the bar letting out a slight sigh, "I'll just have a glass of bourbon." The barkeep nodded as he placed the empty glass down in front of Mavrick and then turned around to look through some of the bottles that he had sitting on a shelf. Grabbing one of the ones off the top shelf, he turned around with the bottle, pulled out the wooden cork, and carefully poured the glass till it was to the brim. "That guy is going to run you Five cents." Mavrick shuffled through his satchel for a moment with his right hand, then handed the barkeep twenty-five cents "Here you go, sir, and please, when this is empty, just keep them coming till you need more money." The Barkeep nodded, taking the money and placing it in the register. With the money secured, he walked to another part of the bar, keeping up with his work, and Mavrick sat there quietly, becoming lost in his drink and thoughts.

What felt like minutes actually became hours; what seemed like one drink became five. Unsure if it was due to the alcohol or the exhaustion, Mavrick started to fall asleep at the bar. This was when the Barkeep came up to him with a gentle smile across his face telling him that he would have to cut him off. Mavrick just nodded, saying, "Yeah, I think I'm done anyway. You got the time by chance?" The barkeep looked at his pocket watch and answered, "Yeah, it's midnight." Mavrick then laughed a little and commented, "So it's High Moon." The barkeep laughed it off and then asked him if he would be okay.

Mavrick nodded as he thanked the barkeep for his hospitality, tipped his hat, and slowly stumbled his way out of the saloon. Once outside the swinging doors, Mavrick sloppily stumbled over toward his horse and worked on unhitching him. With the reins loosened, he started to pull himself up on his horse but stopped when he realized someone down the muddy road was staring at him. "Can I help you, friend?!" Mavrick slurred as he shouted. The figure walked toward him and his horse. "What do you want?!" Mavrick asked loudly, his voice starting to shake a bit, displaying some of the fear that he was feeling. Mavrick then drew his revolvers and aimed them at the figure who was only about three horse lengths away from him. "I'm warning you, stop now and tell me what you want, or I will shoot!" The figure moved slightly closer and stopped where the moonlight shone down upon him. His hands went up in the air, showing surrender, and Mavrick's face became gaunt as his eyes became wide, "I thought you was dead!"

Made in the USA
Columbia, SC
15 June 2025